T0162367

Little Casino

Little asino

GILBERT SORRENTINO

COFFEE HOUSE PRESS

2002

COFFEE HOUSE PRESS is an independent nonprofit literary publisher supported in part by a grant provided by the Minnesota State Arts Board, through an appropriation by the Minnesota State Legislature, and in part by a grant from the National Endowment for the Arts. Significant support was received for this project through a grant from the National Endowment for the Arts, a federal agency, and the Jerome Foundation. Support has also been provided by Athwin Foundation; the Bush Foundation; Buuck Family Foundation; Elmer L. & Eleanor J. Andersen Foundation; Honeywell Foundation; McKnight Foundation; Patrick and Aimee Butler Family Foundation; The St. Paul Companies Foundation, Inc.; the law firm of Schwegman, Lundberg, Woessner & Kluth, P.A.; Marshall Field's Project Imagine with support from the Target Foundation; Wells Fargo Foundation Minnesota; West Group; Woessner-Freeman family Foundation; and many individual donors. To you and our many readers across the country, we send our thanks for your continuing support.

COFFEE HOUSE PRESS books are available to the trade through our primary distributor, Consortium Book Sales & Distribution, 1045 Westgate Drive, Saint Paul, MN 55114. For personal orders, catalogs, or other information, write to: Coffee House Press, 27 North Fourth Street, Suite 400, Minneapolis, MN 55401. Good books are brewing at coffeehousepress.org

LIBRARY OF CONGRESS CATALOGING-IN-PUBLICATION DATA

Sorrentino, Gilbert.
Little Casino / Gilbert Sorrentino.
p. cm.
ISBN 1-56689-126-4 (alk. paper)
1. Brooklyn (New York, N.Y.)—Fiction.
2. Autobiographical memory—Fiction. I. Title.

PS3569.07 L58 2002
813'.54—DC21   2001052943

1 3 5 7 9 10 8 6 4 2
PRINTED IN CANADA

Some sections of this book have appeared in *Conjunctions*, to whose editor the author makes grateful acknowledgment.

When you look through binoculars, you are holding an instrument of precision and you see very clearly a small cabin which would seem quite indistinct without the binoculars. So you say, "Well, well, it's just like another one I know, they are almost alike," and as soon as you say that you no longer see it, in your mind you are comparing it with the one you think came before, *while, in fact, it comes after. Truth means binoculars, precision, the thing that really comes first is the binoculars. You should say, "Well, well, these binoculars are almost the cabin."*

—ROBERT PINGET

Although we may catalogue a kind of chain mysterious is the force that holds the chain together.

—JOSEPH CORNELL

Contents

Little **C**asino

EOPLE ENTER AND THEN INHABIT, HELP-
lessly, periods of their lives during which
they look as if death has spoken to them, or,
even more eerily, as if they themselves are
companions to death. It is not usual for others to notice this in
daily intercourse, but the look is manifest in photographs taken
during these periods.

He and his wife stand side by side in casual summer clothes,
comfortable, and, as they say, contemporary, but in no other way
remarkable. Behind them is a cluttered, even messy kitchen table, in
the center of which, curiously, a tangerine sits atop a coffee mug, and
on the wall behind that is a very poorly done pencil drawing made
by a neighbor's daughter, a senior at the High School of Music and
Art. Such infirm productions attest to the inevitable errors of talent
selection. In the man's face we can see, clearly, the imprint of death
left there years ago by the deaths of his mother and father, who died
less than a year apart. They died badly, as do many people, gasping,
fighting, twitching, their staring eyes registering amazement at how

their bodies were impatiently closing themselves down, literally getting rid of themselves. Enough! Enough!

And then they were gone, they *passed away*. His wife's face has, uncannily, borrowed the subtly peaked, grayish blandness of his own, and so she, too, looks as if she has to do with *the other side*.

But here is another photograph of a middle-aged man, let's say he's the wife's brother, whose eyes, in a placid, contented, almost smug face, have the half-mad, glazed expression which used to be known, among infantrymen, as a thousand-yard stare. Precisely at the spot at which those thousand yards end, or, perhaps, begin, is the more precise word, stands death itself, in mundane disguise, of course, looking like James Stewart in one of his honest-friend roles. The face of the man in the photograph is unsettling, since its peaceful demeanor belies the crazed eyes, which reveal the dark truth. Death, as James Stewart, may have even been approaching when the photograph was taken. Which would go a long way toward explaining the ocular terror.

And here is a group of eight or nine children in a Brooklyn playground in 1959. There are four boys and two girls and they are smiling and mugging with their gap-toothed mouths, their shirts and shorts soaked from the sprinklers whose gossamer spray can be seen in the background. They are enough to break your heart. One of them, a sweet girl with straight black hair, cut short, and with a tiny Miraculous Medal on a chain around her neck, has her hands crossed on her chest. It is this pose which somehow allows access to the expression beneath the sweetness of her lovely face. The occulted expression is the one that can be seen on prisoners in Auschwitz, although this little girl knows nothing of Auschwitz. He puts the photograph down, he *hides* the photograph, but has no true idea why.

Yet the message has been delivered, oh yes. It is at such times that we are brought to consider how completely strange death is, how remote from us, how foreign, how impenetrable, how unfriendly. In its ineradicable distance from our entire experience, it is inhuman.

■ ■ ■

Or: "Death is not an event in life: we do not live to experience death." (6.4311)

Click. Now you see us; now you don't.

Click.

Many people cannot understand why certain religions do not allow animals to enter heaven. Well, we know that they have no souls, but many people wonder about that, too. Do they? When the Rapture snatches Joe Bob Joe outen his Ford pickup, it'll be tough on Mr. Joe to leave Rend and Tear, his "really gentle" Rottweilers, behind.

"Let him change his religion and truly be saved!" Bob Joe Bob says, perhaps irrelevantly.

May their souls and the souls of all the faithful departed, through the mercy of God, rest in peace. Amen. Which implies, maybe, that if God does not wish, in, of course, selected cases, to be merciful, these faithful departed may *not* rest in peace.

Tangerine was, indeed, all they claimed, but she's been dead for about 50 years. Bob Eberle knew her well, and even, so they say, had an amour with her. He may be dead by now as well.

Of what is't fools make such vain keeping?
Sin their conception, their birth weeping,
Their life a general mist of error,
Their death a hideous storm of terror.

John Webster was, clearly, unfamiliar with the rhetoric of grief counseling.

I once heard Ray Eberle, Bob's brother, at the end of his rather undistinguished career, sing in a Brooklyn saloon named Henry's. His backup band was a disastrous trio, piano, accordion, and drums, but he was game. He bummed a cigarette from me at the bar. I was going to tell him that I'd seen him at the Paramount with Glenn Miller, but what was the point?

Click.

ARIO WORE RUBBERS TO SCHOOL EVERY day, for the uppers of his shoes were cracked and split, and the soles worn all the way through. He could have chosen not to wear rubbers, of course, for this was, even in the thirties, America, and freedom, enough to choke a horse, was in the unfailing ascendant. An unkind youth with a belief in his own superiority once thought to bait him about these rubbers, industrial rubbers, as they surely were, slaughterhouse rubbers, with their unmistakable thick red soles. The rage that he saw within Mario's tautly held body dissuaded him, however, and warned him away. A lot of the boys in class, knowing of his plans, were disappointed, because they hoped that maybe Mario would, in the parlance of the day, clean the little bastard's fucking clock. Maybe, God willing, even kill him. Nobody would miss him, least of all the chums of 6B4.

■　■　■

"I wish that all the pain that _____ is feeling could be visited, in spades, on my worst enemy," is a refreshing phrase. If one can't wish one's enemies misery or death, what is the use of sin and redemption?

Follow the leader: Mario, after his bitter childhood years of poverty, which he shared with his older brother, Mike, followed Mike and Mike's wife, Connie, to Trenton, NJ, for God knows what reason. They may still live there, doing the Jersey bounce.

It is generally agreed, or so I understand, that the word "chum" is no longer in general use, save for ironic or parodic affect. It functions, that is, much like the well-made short story.

"Of which we've read, ah, plenty."

E TAKES BUBBSY, WHOM HE HATES, BUT HAS no idea why, up to the roof, for reasons never explained, reasons never even suggested by the quiet, handsome boy, who has lived, more or less, in saloons most of his life. His mother has kept him in food and clothes, despite the fact that she rarely leaves the bar, save to stagger into the ladies' room with one drunken lothario or another. He pulls Bubbsy, by the hair, to the edge of the roof, and throws him off. Bubbsy lands on a Studebaker coupe, crushing the roof with his head, which cracks open in a mess of blood and brains. He leans over the edge of the roof and lights a cigarette, then carefully drops a burnt match, aiming at the body, but the wind blows the match well off line and out of sight. He thinks that the coupe belongs to that stupid prick who lives over the candy store on the corner. That would be nice.

■　■　■

Hide and seek: death. He had been in Lincoln Hall. After the death of Bubbsy, he was sent to Coxsackie, then Dannemora. Nobody knew where he went from there, although there were recurring, preposterous rumors that he was acting in the movies, with a different face.

"They can do fuckin' anything in Hollywood."

Bubbsy liked to torture cats and cruelly tease and hurt little children. Had he lived, there is a good chance that he would have become a hail-fellow-well-met regular sport of a bully, drunk, and dedicated beater of women, like his older brother, Mac, the cop.

"There are always, sure, a few bad apples in the barrel, but it's very wrong to condemn and blacken all the other honest, hardworking, law-abiding people who and so forth, and who and so on, and who, day in and day out, do this and do that and do the other thing too."

It could happen to you. Hide. And seek.

The same darkness envelops them all.

AVE A SPAGHETTI SANGWICH! HAVE A
spaghetti sangwich with pieces of cold
frankfurter on it! Have a cod-liver oil sandwich, a sammich that'll put hair on your
chest, your head, your hands, and your freezing feet!

A ketchup sammich? A ketchup-and-mustard sammich? Or
how does a cold stringbean sammich strike you, little fella? A
canned pineapple sandwich might go well with a big jelly jar
chock by Jesus Christ up to the brim with lemon Epco or grape
Kool-Aid, as too might a canned-spinach sandwich. Succotash
on moldy rye? Mmmm.

A cottage-cheese-and-cold-boiled-puhtaytuh sangaweech on
stale Bond bread, now that is the absolute ticket! You're talking
nutrition? Then, too, sandwiches of sliced green pepper and
Crisco will surely refresh after a long day of career discussions.
And don't neglect to pop over to friendly Gallagher's, sport, for a
pitcher of Trommer's: crisp, light, and tingling! And zesty! It's the
Ivy League beverage of choice, you'll recall?

How to feed your family of five, or even six, on a dollar a day, without endangering their health or welfare. Just takes a little g-u-m-p gumption!

Stay away, oh, stay far hence from those terrible crumb buns, cinnamon buns, coconut buns, crullers, doughnuts, and Danish pastries: they'll send you to your grave, yowzah.

Break out the lettuce-and-oleo sammiches, pliz. Look at those smiling children in the sunny kitchen! Look at those cavities and suppurating ears! Bacon and eggs and sausages and toast with butter, again! That will do it every time.

Afterward, when the coughing lets up a little, these tykes can build a little character selling *Liberty* at the subway station. "How to Feed Your Growing Family on Fifty Cents a Day" is in the latest issue, wow!

And for the love of God, who does not cotton to the idle poor, as we all know, *please* avoid those thick steaks, buttered mashed potatoes, rich sauces, cream-laden desserts, all those deadly foods that will damage the courageous heart, OK?

Lard on toast might allay certain yearnings, but moderation, moderation.

How amazing that the poor have *always* eaten a healthy diet, rich in vegetables, legumes, and whole grains, and low in fat and sugars. They've had it puh-retty darn good!

Here you go—a kohlrabi sangwich on what looks like a fetching pale-green slice of Silvercup! Fulla vitamins Q and T.

■ ■ ■

Herbert Hoover died at the age of 137, of course. It is said that he never ate a steak in his life, and that his favorite dinner was farmer cheese on soda crackers with skim milk.

He did *not* call the unemployed "the shiftless idle," and the rumor that attributed this remark to him has been traced to Ethel and Julius Rosenberg, described as "Godless un-Cristian [sic] Jews" in *Jesus Knows News*. It is a cruel rumor, and one that is in very poor taste as well.

When the burdens of the Depression and such aberrations as the Bonus March could not be lightened by cheery thoughts of Tom Mix, Mr. Hoover often went fly-fishing, called "the sport of dukes." He wore his Stanford tie.

"Don't fence me in!" the doughty President would exultantly cry to the aromatic woods. And soon it would be time for a raw onion.

ESOLATE LOT. A BOY OF PERHAPS FOUR, in a tattered and patched hand-me-down windbreaker, a knitted cap on his head against the raw cold of a late March afternoon. He is alone, rooting with a stick in the rubble of broken red and buff bricks, shards of stained porcelain, diseased shingles, tree limbs, all the rubbish and detritus of this failing neighborhood, struggling for life on the thinnest edge of utter decay. It is the very picture of loneliness. The boy's father, who has gone to look for him as the bitter darkness begins to slide across the low roofs of the neighborhood houses, watches him, heartbrokenly, in silence. He knows, although he has no idea that he knows, that the boy, alone in the sad quiet of this gray, dispirited lot, will be alone always in his life, and that the distant, perplexing world that he is to inhabit is one to which he will be forever strange. This knowledge enters the father with viral efficiency, and years later, he will remember this day, even remember the shape of a brown leaf that lies at his feet, crepitant.

And years later, after a long period of estrangement and silence, the boy, now a solitary man, will write his father a letter, suggesting that the years of separation and misunderstanding might, possibly, be ended, might, possibly, be "cured," is his odd word. And the father, tentatively, carefully, replies, with guarded love and exquisite care, but hopelessly. The boy will have no memory of the death of hope that lay at the center of that lot, at the center of that raw afternoon, eerie in thin, failing sunlight and dirty cold. The father will have no way of telling his son of the truth that was thrust upon him, as he watched from the sidewalk before he called to him to come home. The fact of the loveless void of that shattered lot on that unremarkable block in Brooklyn in the fading years of the 1950s will be in and of his letter, and even as he mails it, the letter, full of carefully phrased sentences that demand nothing and expect nothing and promise nothing, that is but a salute, labored yet authentic, will not, he knows, be answered.

■ ■ ■

Céline writes that "the living people we've lost in the crypts of time sleep so soundly side by side with the dead that the same darkness envelops them all."

No one used to think that a vacant lot was *owned,* rather, lots were everybody's property, loci of quiet anarchy. A lot took its character from that of the surrounding neighborhood. Because of this, it was an accurate index of a neighborhood's present, but held no hint of its future. To place a living human figure in the center of a lot is to *compose* a kind of iconic reality that is, oddly, more real than the presence of an actual living figure in the center of a lot.

It is hard to be a father.

No love. No nothing.

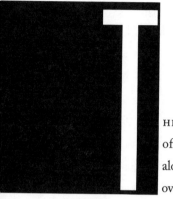

HE BOY LEAPS FROM THE SLIPPERY EDGE of the pier out toward the scow tied up alongside it. He's done this dozens of times over the past few years, timing the slow heave and slide of the clumsy vessel as the swells carry it toward the pier and then away from it, but this time he misjudges and, in midair, his arms outstretched and his legs pistoning, realizes that he won't land on the deck. His left foot touches the gunwale, but the scow is riding away from him on the water, glassy with oil. Some other boys stand in momentary silent terror, still, on the pier in the anemic sunlight and brisk wind of the October afternoon, knowing that their friend's foot has not gained purchase. He falls between the hull and the pier just as the scow reaches its maximum distance from the pier, and is held, wholly still, by its huge, splintery hawsers. As the boy surfaces, the scow lifts and begins its terrible slide toward him, the swell carrying it silently, calmly, toward the pier. A deckhand hears the screaming of the boys on the pier and emerges, half-drunk, from a makeshift cabin of planks and tarpaper on the deck, and knows, instantly, what has happened, and that there is nothing to be done. He stands at the gunwale and looks into the space between the hull and the pier, sees the boy's small, tough face white with shock and fear, and yells, in a voice high with rage and anguish, in a near-comic Norwegian accent, that the focking goddamn kid is focking goddamn crazy and to get the focking goddamn hell out of there, and then the boy is a soft crack and an explosion of gore and, weirdly, makes no sound as he is crushed to his filthy death.

■　■　■

"What did you see as you fell? What did you hear as you sank?/Did it make you drunken with hearing?"

The boy would not have understood these lines in any other way but the literal. That is, had anyone known to avail him of the poem from which they come. But who would have known?

Go fish. And blues in the night.

O BOMBARD THE SMALL AND INEFFICIENT gas refrigerator with grapefruit would be his weekly, perhaps daily delight, yet he was astigmatic, myopic, amblyopic, cross-eyed, knock-kneed, bowlegged, and box-ankled. To heave huge turkeys, each shot several times with a .38 caliber Smith & Wesson revolver, into the kitchen sink, seemed a promising idea, not, however, to be realized by the likes of him, who could not catch a ball, the pitiful bastard. To pull up the skirts and slips of all the pretty girls on their way to Sunday mass was a romantic ideal, and yet, he broke his steel clinic glasses every week or so. What about throwing the guys who had ripped his shirt right off the fucking roof, one after the other? But had he ever, once, managed to hit the ball past the infield? Killing that large, handsome German shepherd with a perfect slab of perfectly poisoned meat would have surely benefited mankind, but the poor chooch was afraid to put his head underwater. To become a priest, kind and brave and strong among the disgusting yet worthy lepers, was a noble calling, but how could he find time to study when he couldn't stop polluting himself for a minute, the pasty-faced, underweight, nervous degenerate? He could easily kidnap Dolores and Georgene from in front of Fontbonne Hall and carry them off to Rio and CARNIVAL! and unspeakable sin, although he would not let them know that he still, on occasion, wet the bed. To sink, with nary a moment's hesitation, the Staten Island ferry, so as to drown the secret Nazi agents who spied on convoys in the Narrows would have shortened the war by a month, but he was having serious problems with long division. To use his Amazing Hypnotic Powers, from time to time, and solely for the refined amusement of his closest academic chums, so as to compel Miss Ramsay to happily strip naked in front of the hearty group gathered in the detention room was a pastime that appealed to his sense of fair play, but hard, hard to do when she pinched his earlobe and called him a dunce. To smoke a quiet pipe before the cheery fire while mulling over the details of the latest gruesome ax murder always hit the old anglophilic spot, but not for the sort of rough fellow who smoked Wings, Twenty Grand, and Sweet Caporal loosies. To show Liz and Mary how to do the Harlem Glide could have been a charming way to pass the time, had the young women been willing to tolerate the importunate if unintentional prodding of his manly erection. He argued, convincingly, that a Tom Collins was more refreshing than a John Collins, that upstart drink, but his buttocks showed through the large holes in his threadbare corduroy knickers. And who better to warn the grizzled pilots of the *Queen Mary* and the *Normandy,* as the great ships approached the Narrows, of the foul Sargasso Sea of floating condoms that threatened their safety? But had not two Garfield Boys cut his tie off with a switchblade and stolen his lunch money? To batter the persons of the neighborhood bullies, in, of course, strict accordance with the Rules of the Ring, while casually remarking on Annette's tiny though shapely breasts, was always invigorating, but the shirt-cardboard inserts in his worn-out shoes were soaked through. To carry swiftly messages of highest priority, down pitch-black streets, from one air-raid warden to another, could help to bring the Axis to its knees, but 3¢ chocolate sodas and Mrs. Wagner's strangely malevolent pies had given him a faceful of pimples. Most seriously, he would have liked to explode a magical bomb that he had invented one night in bed, a bomb that would do the Job, that is, maim, dismember, roast, fry, broil, and obliterate all his enemies, but for the fact that a group of charming and brilliant, sober and judicious proxy killers were about to do the trick. Twice.

■ ■ ■

Turkeys that have been shot, however accurately, with .38 caliber slugs, are not edible. A man named Pasquale Colluccio demonstrated this fact to me when I was sixteen, and to my complete satisfaction.

In Brooklyn, in what many people have been taught by crack journalists to call "a more innocent time," floating condoms were often called "Coney Island whitefish," whereas condoms discarded on the ground after use were, quite simply, "scumbags," semen being, of course, "scum." Bodies torn apart by bullets fired into them at close range were often come upon in vacant lots in Bath Beach and Canarsie. "Hello! There's Santo Throckmorton, the jewel thief!" The occasional newborn infant would be fished out, dead as Santo, from ashcans filled with clinkers and "scumbags," or recovered from the ladies' room in the Alpine, Stanley, Electra, Bay Ridge, Dyker, and Harbor.

An "ashcan" was the name given to a very large and powerful firecracker, responsible, each Fourth of July, for the loss of the fingers and eyes of many neighborhood youths. These occurrences might be placed under the heading of "Good Practice" for the good and righteous war that was just around the cozy little corner. We showed *them*.

It is often forgotten that they also showed us.

Someone, after Hiroshima, was reported to have remarked, anent the scientists who had created the bomb: What did they *think* was going to happen when it exploded?

"Music? Music? Music?"

FTER AN HOUR OR SO OF TRYING TO GET
her brassiere off, or her skirt up, or both, he
lies back, next to her, on the couch, thinking that maybe he'll just go home, when
she accidentally brushes, with the back of her hand, and through
his slacks, his still-erect but by now leaden penis, and he realizes
that he's going to come. It's like a joke. Let's say, unequivocally,
that it *is* a joke.

Some ten years later, the boy, now, of course, a man, very
drunk but not so drunk as his wife, spreads her legs open as they
lie, he is somewhat surprised to realize, on the living room car-
peting. She is humming, over and over, the first bar of "Ruby, My
Dear." He cannot understand, for the life of him, and it's not, let's
face it, much of a life, why he is unable to pull her panties any further down than her thighs. Can't make a fucking thing *right* anymore, he says to her, but she pays him no mind, or, in any event,
she does not reply. Then he puts his head on her naked belly and
they both fall asleep.

And, lest it be forgotten, there is his first serious sexual experience, when a nurse or a nurse's aide at Brooklyn Eye and Ear, where he lies after an operation, both eyes bandaged, feeds him his supper, tells him what she looks like, and, while spooning what may be tapioca pudding into his mouth, masturbates him under the covers with skill and dispatch. He thinks that he might faint with pleasure, but he stays marvelously conscious, even alert, listening to the rustle of what he imagines to be her crisp white uniform.

As she is leaving the room, she says, mysteriously, "There are a lot of nice guys in Jersey, too, but."

■   ■   ■

One might, as an amusement, do worse than to think of adventures such as these enveloping forward-looking politicians, dim professors of civil engineering, and dreadful Christian fundamentalists. (Add or substitute your own favorites.)

It is the fashion to make fun of New Jersey, much as it is the fashion to denigrate Los Angeles and to praise the San Francisco Bay Area. "What weather!" they bubble, as the earth splits open amid vast fires, and the houses slide downhill, in cataracts of mud, onto the clogged and poisonous freeways.

Sexual experiences are rarely reported with candor, accuracy, or honesty, and these are no exceptions.

Why is this the case? It's magic?

In 1968, CBS wanted Thelonious Monk to record an album of Beatles tunes. There sat the band's songbook on his piano. To add, as the nice phrase has it, insult to injury, the company sent someone to Monk's apartment to play through the book. In case Monk couldn't read music.

Well, you needn't, motherfucker.

PHOTOGRAPH OF DOLORES IN PROSPECT Park. She is in a dusty-rose suit and has on a small white hat with a half-veil, white gloves, blush-tan nylons, and white high heels. Behind her are Mary and Liz. In another photograph we discover Dolores and Georgene, the latter in a pale-yellow suit with matching gloves and a flat straw hat, white heels. Annette is beside her, too, her face in half-profile, laughing, one hand holding down her light beige skirt, which the wind is lifting, slightly, above her knees. Their teeth seem remarkably white, their figures just beginning to take on womanly contours. It must be Easter Sunday, let us assume that it is Easter Sunday. On the back of a photograph of Dolores—yet another one, in which she poses dramatically against a lamppost—someone has written, in a labored, childish hand, "sweet young girl."

■   ■   ■

Time. The photographs, somewhat carelessly and inadequately described here, are in black and white.

"Photographs, because they exclude everything except the split second in which they are snapped, always lie," he once wrote. Time.

And the angels sing, but perhaps not always.

Dusty rose, pale yellow, and light beige were spring colors, worn exclusively by virgins. Don't argue with me!

ONALD SMIRKS AND TELLS THE FOOL THAT Liz told him, and that Mary, Liz's best friend, told her, and that she, Mary, heard it from Georgene, who goes to Fontbonne Hall *with* Dolores, that she, Dolores, sometimes changes, after physical education class, into black lace underwear, garments that look, according to Georgene, like sin itself, garments that have been proscribed by the Pope, garments that the nuns have forbidden the girls even to think about, on pain of mortal sin.

The fool can no longer look at dark, tall, shy Dolores without having the urge to say or do something so idiotically reprehensible that the neighborhood will never forget it, even unto the tenth generation.

The fool can't talk to Dolores without blushing.

The fool can't think of Dolores without committing the terrible sin of self-abuse that will send him to hell soon after he loses his health and sanity and life. But Dolores will also be in hell, oh Jesus Christ, and naked, like everybody else. God must be out of his mind.

The fool thinks about talking to Donald concerning this vile tale, but Donald is a thickheaded lump of a boy, ravaged by acne, meanness, and varied budding pathologies, and would, the fool knows, probably snicker and grab at his crotch in overt insult to the dark goddess.

One day, when the fool sees Dolores skipping rope with Mary and Liz, the snowy whiteness of her slip glancing out, each time she skips, from under her navy-blue jumper, he realizes that he will probably collapse and die if he can't stop thinking of Dolores standing, nervously blushing and trembling, in nothing but her black lace underwear, the specific configuration of which he cannot imagine. Just as well. A few minutes later, as the girls start for home and supper, Dolores approaches the fool and asks him if he'd like to keep her company on the following Thursday night when she baby-sits for the Ryans. He nods, from out of the darkness of erotic mania that has enshrouded him. That would be nice, he says, sure, he says, to the impossibly lovely and amazingly half-naked girl who is smiling at him. His hands at his side are, what are they? They are cauliflowers, much too big to put into his stupid pockets.

■ ■ ■

Mount St. Vincent's Academy, St. Mary's Academy, Cathedral Girls', Bishop McDonnell Memorial. Each has at least one Dolores among their various student bodies. "Such is the way of Satan and his clever wiles, boys."

There is no proscription, in the teachings of the Roman Catholic Church, against the wearing of black lace underwear. If such apparel should become the occasion of sin, however, well, you're on your own.

Donald, you will not be surprised to know, was secretly in love with

Dolores, of course. He often whispered her name as he punched himself in the mouth. What the hell happened to your face, Don?

Donald liked to eat chocolate-covered graham crackers covered with grape jelly, and adorned with chopped-up marshmallows, all washed down with Dixie Shake. His acne sang the song of empty gratification.

To think that God might be out of his mind is blasphemous. On the other hand, is it blasphemous to think that God might occasionally wear a dusty-rose suit? A string of pearls?

"You're on dangerous ground, boys, with a thought like that, just what the foul fiend likes to see."

"La volupté unique et suprême de l'amour gît dans la certitude de faire le mal."

OLORES, DARK, BLACK-EYED, SWEET ITAL-
ian girl, with a straight-A average at
Fontbonne Hall, who looks absolutely
beautiful in her school uniform, asks him if
he'd like to come over to the Ryans' apartment to keep her company while she's baby-sitting. Her breasts are too small—just as well—for her to wear a brassiere, but lovely beneath her snowy, spotless blouse.

He sees that the Ryans have a piano in the living room, a small upright that, he will soon discover, is utterly out of tune. They drink Cokes, they eat peanut-butter sandwiches, and then Dolores, he's certain, looks directly into his face and tells him that she's wearing black lace underwear. He thinks that he probably hasn't heard this, so he grins and says—what savoir faire!— "What?" She says, he is certain that she says, "I know you won't believe me, you're such a dope, but I'm wearing, *really*, black lace underwear." Just as he's about to do something crazed and reckless, he has no idea what, perhaps pull up her skirt or kiss her white anklets, she smiles, drapes, for some arcane reason, a towel over his head, and sits down at the piano. She plays, mechanically, the tinny piano making the music sinister, "All or Nothing at All." One of the straps of her jumper slips off her shoulder and he buries his face in the towel. He cannot look at her and he cannot think of her and he cannot say her name. Even the towel is making him crazy.

■   ■   ■

"Just as well," in the context of this faux-vignette, or, perhaps more accurately, Catholic joke, means "just as well," and only "just as well."

Dolores became a registered nurse.

"Haunted heart," a malady with which this "dope" was afflicted, has an *almost* comic or melodramatic ring to it, especially when paired with "registered nurse." Can't be helped.

Many of the boys and young men in the neighborhood thought that Dolores's nose was too big, and made crude and vulgar comments about her. These comments issued from those who had driven themselves senseless with pink-and-white fantasies concerning blondes like Doris Day, June Allyson, and Virginia Mayo, women who, it might fairly be argued, were virtually noseless. Dolores's nose was the nose of Clodia and Lesbia, of Sulpicia and Cynthia. Of Helen.

"If hair is mussed on her forehead, if she goes in a gleam of Cos, in a slither of dyed stuff, there is a volume in the matter."

And if her skin smells of Castile soap, he "shall spin long yarns out of nothing," and sing them to the dreadful noise of an out-of-tune piano.

The light of bowling alleys

E HAD BEEN VAGUELY AWARE, FOR SOME time, that odd and unexpected things often happened in odd and unexpected places, but he had no sense that such things could happen to him. Perry or Sam, let's say Perry, had picked him up about seven o'clock, after supper, in his old dusty black Plymouth coupe, and they'd gone up the hill to the Blue Front for a Coke, then down to Chez Freddy, if witnesses can be believed, but nobody seemed to be around. Well, it was a May weekend, well before the season. They wound up in, of all places, the bowling alley. He didn't know how to bowl and Perry wasn't much good, but they rented their shoes and made fools of themselves: expected behavior for bowling alleys. A few people were there, and a couple of girls, the bowling-alley light, harsh and shadowless, setting them in clattering and crashing space precisely. The light of bowling alleys can be proven romantic, though the steps of the proof and its final flourish may be too simple to be given credence.

He had no idea where her Evander Childs High School was, nor her Boston Post Road, nor her Mosholu Parkway, Van

Cortlandt Park, Gun Hill Road, but these were mysterious places to which she *belonged*, and were strangely inextricable, too, in his wayward mind, from the crisp white uniforms worn by nurses, from the perfume-edged odor of sweat, or so he was compelled to believe, even from the smell of ice-cold furs and the oil-slicked glassy waters of the Narrows. He knew that something was happening, despite the banality of everything, perhaps because of the banality of everything, the musty smell of the garage, just opened after the winter, the dirty screens leaning against the sides of the house, awaiting springtime cleaning, the blowing phlox bordering the hedge. There she stood. He looked around for Perry, Perry Plymouth, where was he? and he was talking to the other girl, small and dark, with startlingly white, even teeth and a short haircut that held her face in an ebony frame. Later, that summer, his friend, Teddy, would fall in love with this dark girl, making his Italian family as unhappy as her Jewish family. "Such goeth the breaks, brother mine," Teddy's older brother, Joe, would say, but sadly. In any event, what was happening to *him*, now, could well be considered instrumental in understanding the romantic nature of bowling-alley light. Which, by curious but logical divagation, which there is no time to explain, led him to wonder, that summer, about the whereabouts of Perry.

Helen, her older sister, picked him up at the DeCamp bus stop in Caldwell that fall, in their father's car, a powder-blue Buick. What in God's name was he doing at the Caldwell bus stop? In the fall? Helen was engaged to a second-year medical student, Sam, whom she'd met at Jones Beach. Of him and her younger sister, Sam had said, that past August, "You sly dog." Which reminds me that Marvin, her cousin, had said, "If she weren't my cousin, oh yeah, oh Jesus."

■ ■ ■

The subject of the foregoing is not at all clear, as will be obvious to the attentive reader. The subject, for all I know, may not even be in evidence.

$$R = \frac{2\pi^2 m b^4}{\lambda^3}$$

Werner Heisenberg was not convinced by this proof, and thought it, as a matter of fact, "frivolous." But then Heisenberg had no idea of what a bowling alley is, or, in this case, was. He is on record as saying, in reply to a question concerning bowling alleys, posed him by Lotte Knapke, "Of that which I cannot talk about, I have to keep my mouth quiet." He of course meant "silent."

It's perfectly OK for New Yorkers to make fun of New Jersey and/or its residents, but it is not OK for others to do so. And I mean New Yorkers, not transplanted rubes like, say, E.B. White.

"What about a transplanted rube like Virgil Thomson?"

Fuck him, too, with his wand and his peanut-butter pie!

"I'm not quite . . . ?"

Wand, wand, *wand,* for Christ sake! You never heard of a wand, and pie?

"You mean maybe a cane?"

HE NIGHT BEFORE, HE HAD WALKED HER to her house down by the lake. Thick sweet darkness of the July night. He kissed her, leaning against the cool metal of her father's powder-blue Buick. She said that she'd see him down at the lake the next day. I've seen you there, a lot, she said, last year.

And there she was the next day, lying on a blanket some twenty-five yards from the pavilion, with a girlfriend. She looked up at him and smiled. Do I know you? she said. He felt like a shambling moron in the face of that candid, girlish smile, and the girlfriend was giving him the once-over. Do you, like a, want a, like a want to have Coke? he said. She laughed and got up on her knees and patted the blanket with a hand so golden that her fingernails glowed as pearls. Here, she said. Sit here. He looked at her cool lips and felt them again in the moonless night.

The jukebox in the pavilion was playing a cheap song that would become ludicrously and unimpeachably beautiful in years to come, and the girlfriend left. Lie down, she said. I had a bad feeling that you weren't going to say hello. What? What? Wasn't it obvious from his stricken and stupid face that his very self had become her imbecile and slave? He saw that her eyes were hazel.

■　■　■

For heaven's sake, it's too soon to know. But it's magic, tenderly. So said Claude Thornhill, Fran Warren, Dinah Washington, Doris Day, Sarah Vaughan.

She wore a white, one-piece strapless bathing suit.

Complexity of the simplest things, e.g., young men and women, or this young man and this young woman.

It doesn't matter what lake in New Jersey this was. They were all alike. It doesn't matter what the girl's name was. They were all lovely.

Hopatcong, Ellen, Budd, Natalie, Hiawatha, Carole.

"I'll close my eyes and she'll just disappear, I know it, I know it," the idiot says. To himself, at *least.*

LTHOUGH INFORMATION, SPARSE AND unsatisfactory as it is, has been grudgingly offered by crack journalists as to the mundane origins of a mundane summer romance that began in, of all places, a mundane bowling alley, the activities of Perry have been all but ignored, not only on that particular night (of the bowling alley), but throughout the entirety of the subsequent summer.

Questions were asked, possible witnesses canvassed, and so on. No one seems to remember Perry's activities.

Perry was seen, as we know, in conversation with the small, dark girl, and we have been told, perhaps irrelevantly, that "later that summer, his [not Perry's] friend, Teddy, would fall in love with [her]." Did Perry also fall in love with her? Did he tell her of *his* notions concerning the romantic light of bowling alleys? What actually *happened* to Perry that summer? For that matter, what happened to him that *night?* All the information so far granted or gathered has been filtered through a prose utterly, even slavishly subservient to the sensibilities of an embarrassingly lovestruck young man, dazed by a girl, by her smile and her perfume, and by the concomitant and irregularly recurring image of a faceless female body in what he imagines to be a crisp white uniform. Can such a prose be trusted? Was Perry angry that the small, dark girl found, if that's the word, Teddy? And if there was such anger, did Teddy ever learn of it? Did Perry despise himself for his amorous vacillation, procrastination, shyness?

Somebody supposedly remarked to Hal, who would be killed the following summer in an automobile crash near the Delaware Water Gap, that Perry had been in Caldwell on, it was clear, the same fall afternoon that the young man, stupid with love, was picked up at the bus stop in that little town by the girl's older sister, Helen. The small, dark-haired girl was also at the lake on that crisp, chilly weekend, but she was with two Upsala freshmen, Bob and Noah, complacent and insufferable identical twins destined for contented, more or less, lives, defined by endodontics, corporate law, and marital infidelities. She and Teddy had broken up; the young man, "our hero," if you please, would soon break up with the girl of the bowling alley and beach and smooth tan.

But what on earth had Perry been doing in Caldwell?

He wished, for a long time afterward, that he could meet Perry again, bump into him somewhere, and explain. Explain? Explain what?

He went back to the lake years later, but he might as well have gone to Akron or Sunnyvale or Killeen. He stood outside a Radio Shack that had been the Blue Front. He stood there for an hour, smoking. Was he waiting for Perry? Maybe. Or Teddy? Or the magical girl in the white bathing suit? The bowling alley had also been torn down, and on its site was a buffet restaurant, Jack's Pantry. Just as well.

■　■　■

This area of New Jersey was served by two bus lines, the DeCamp Bus Lines and the gray-and-white municipal buses of the Public Service.

It is always safe to poke fun at dentists, as the motion-picture business, in all its creative brilliance, well knows.

"Obviously, the author 'well knows' it, too."

Perhaps Helen picked him up in a Chrysler station wagon: they still had wooden sides in 1948. Perhaps he made love to Helen in the back of the station wagon. Or maybe she drove them to a . . . maison de rendezvous.

"A maison de rendezvous? In Essex County, New Jersey?"

The beginner, bowling, looks somewhat endearing, but when shooting pool, he appears to be bumblingly incompetent, lost and abandoned and foolish. This proves that pool is a real game.

It is always safe to poke fun at bowling, as any fifth-rate stand-up comic knows. And when bowling won't get a laugh, there's always the toilet, humping, waitresses, and stupid girlfriends.

"It can be, kind folk, a veritable laff riot."

If you have ever sojourned in Fort Hood, Texas, the chances are good that you whiled away many an evening in the town of Killeen.

"Your notions, Perry, concerning the romantic light of bowling alleys?"

"R equals two pi squared times em bee to the fourth power over lambda to the third power, lady."

HE TAPIOCA WAS, LET'S ASSUME, WILDLY
sweet in his dream, and the girl was smiling
a lasciviously pure smile, although her face
was not quite clear. She was wearing a crisp
white uniform. The touch of her hand, the firmness and warmth
of her thigh against his, the weight of her body on the bed, her
quick and expert hand. She held a starched napkin for him to
come into. She didn't come back the next day nor the next and
then his father came and took him out of the hospital, both eyes
still bandaged.

They got into his father's Cadillac, around them an early fall
clarity of sound, and a sharpness to the light wind in the trees on
quiet Parkside Avenue.

In the woman's apartment, Connie, his father called her, he
guided him to a chair at the kitchen table. Connie's voice was
something like the voice of the girl in the hospital. She gave
him a 7 Up and he held the cold bottle, listening to sounds of
lovemaking behind a closed door, whispers and small sighs, for

maybe a half-hour, but then his father said, in a very harsh voice, that he wanted the goddamned furs back, did she think that he meant for her to keep them, just a dime-a-dozen skirt like she was?

They walked down the stairs, his father holding his arm and steering him carefully. They could both hear her crying behind the apartment door, but said nothing. The furs were soft and cool against his hand. There's no need for your mother to know we stopped off, his father said, it's just business. The kid got confused, but she's a smart girl, went to Manhattan Marymount to be a dietician. She's got a crackerjack of a sister.

He thought to ask his father if she worked, maybe, part-time at the hospital, but knew that it was stupid and that she didn't. The girl at the hospital was sweet and understood how much he wanted her to touch him. Connie was a tramp. His father dialed the radio to some dance music. The furs smelled like fresh air and perfume, they smelled like women. So you want to swing by Nathan's for a coupla hot dogs, eagle-eye? his father said, and squeezed his thigh.

■   ■   ■

Stories of promiscuity on the part of nurses and nurses' aides in hospitals and clinics are, of course, legion, and some are absolutely true.

"How many?"

About 2.76333%.

Then the woman in the white silk pants suit at the bar says to him, "This is really too good to be true! Aren't you the guy who had that wonderfully surprising and gratifying sexual experience in Caledonia Hospital in Brooklyn back in 1945? Well, I'm not *that* girl, but on the other hand, look at me!" [So it wasn't Brooklyn Eye and Ear.]

Q. What is more boring than a costume party? And yet, here they are, "getting ready," as the phrase has it, to go to one. He is a Filthy Capitalist, oh Jesus Christ spare us, with top hat, cigar, and bulky canvas bag adorned with a dollar sign; and his wife is a Bossy Nurse, help!, with huge horn-rimmed glasses, thick-soled shoes, and clipboard. When they get back home, he follows her into the bedroom, then holds her in his arms as tremblingly and self-revealingly as Melville's Pierre first held Isabel. He lifts her white nylon skirt with sober passion, and she pushes her belly against him. "Oh, sweetheart, oh, sweetheart," she says. She is terribly excited, as is he, and yet he says, looking directly into her dark eyes, "Don't throw bouquets at me."

This is sometimes known as *putting the kibosh on things*. It is followed by his wife's:

"God! Let me get out of this damned uniform! How do those nurses wear these tacky things?"

All over for the nonce.

Stories of costume parties at which people actually do become other people are few and far between, but mostly true.

A. English Department meetings at any American university or college.

To get this young wife "out of [her] damned uniform" is not at all the same thing as having her undress.

Tu-whit, tu-whoo, jug-jug, and ding-a-ding.

HORTS AND DRESSES. AND SKIRTS AND blouses.

And shirts and slips and half-slips and camisoles.

And brassieres and panties and corsets and girdles and teddies. And garter belts, sheer stockings, high heels.

Suits, evening gowns, slacks, jeans. Christ knows what else, or what they're called. Dozens, scores, hundreds, thousands of each article of clothing, lacy and silky and soft and smooth and shining, mountains of the stuff, miles of it. Hats.

But not a single woman to be discovered in any one of these things, not one, anywhere. This, says Father Graham to himself, is the libertine's hell, or should be, at least it's mine. His eyes are looking at something that is not in the rectory, his eyes are glassy, yet frightened. The liquefaction of her clothes, he says, and moans. Help me, God, help me.

■　■　■

"O how that glittering taketh me!" O! O! O!

This "Father Graham," surely the figment, the crude figment of a particularly diseased imagination, does not in any way represent the loving, serene, chaste, and paternal shepherd whom millions of the faithful have honored and will continue to honor as the true bulwark of Holy Mother Church: Joseph Cardinal Cullinane.

"O my God! I am heartily sorry for having offended Thee, and I detest all my sins, because I dread the loss of heaven and the pains of hell, but most of all because I have offended Thee, my God, Who art all good and deserving of all my love. I firmly resolve, with the help of Thy grace, to confess my sins, to do penance, and to amend my life. Amen."

It is, perhaps, just as well that Father Graham has sublimated his tormenting desires into simple fetishes, since the parish is filled with women in their actual flesh.

Their flesh, he whispers, in the dark. Their sinful flesh!

Beauty Parade

T FIFTEEN, DURING THE CRUSHINGLY slow months of the numbingly lonely vacations that his family spends at the lake, he discovers, one day, over at the Lang house, dozens of copies of *Beauty Parade*, dating back five years or so, leafs through the pages of big luscious women, all rich curves and swelling flesh pushing out of the tight, astonishingly abbreviated costumes that have not, surely, words adequate to describe them. And amid the sliding and mildewed piles of newspapers, magazines, junk statuary, empty whiskey bottles, fishing lures and spoons and hooks, sinkers and floats, and cartons, half-cartons, and opened packs of Lord Salisbury cigarettes, he learns to lust and to smoke.

Orville and Jackie Lang, old bachelor brothers, who allow anyone the run of their house and the raw, half-finished workshop behind it when they're away at work, have unwittingly introduced this boy to the twin, darkly scintillant vices of self-abuse and smoking, two wondrous hells which he luxuriously inhabits. Orville owns a flat-bottomed rowboat, painted a bright, harsh, somehow sinful green, which is moored under the rusting footbridge at the end of the road leading to a small island, the keys to its padlock, along with its oars, just behind the door to the workshop. Each afternoon, all that thickly hot summer, our youthful lecher masturbates himself into nirvana at picture after picture of these utterly generous and unashamed, sensual women, who smile directly at him from out of their welter of lace and satin and elastic, of nylon and patent leather, then he smokes a Lord Salisbury, takes two more, and prepares to spend the balance of the afternoon rowing down the little river to the lake, where he drifts in its center, smoking his stolen cigarettes and listening to the voices and laughter of the young people, whom he does not know and whom he desperately envies, slide out to him in faint timbre from the far-off beach.

In three years' time, he will fall in love with one of the girls who sat, that very summer, on that beach with her sister and mother, a girl whom he will meet through, somehow, a casual friend, Perry? He and this girl will often cross the footbridge to the deserted and overgrown island where, their young flesh sweating, they will drive each other mad in the dark. He will not comment to her on the rowboat, nor, of course, on the delirium of his lost afternoons, when, kneeling amid the hardly credible mountains of junk and trash at the Langs', he showed his complaisant harem what he was made of! And in three years' time, he will know the words for each item of underwear worn by those women, women who patiently wait for his unlikely return. The girl that he will adore will not, of course, wear the wondrously tawdry garments of his courtesans. Such is life.

And, in three years' time, he will occasionally sit, in early twilight, with Orville, and accept a Lord Salisbury, even though he smokes Philip Morris. Jackie will emerge from the disaster of a house in a vast reek of Aqua Velva to climb into his black Chrysler convertible and start up the hill for a night of drinking and dancing with yet another graying widow who can, as Jackie always says, "ball that goddamned jack." But he will be uncomfortable with Orville, and, soon, will stop passing the occasional hour or so with him altogether.

■ ■ ■

The winter before this youth met the girl with the honey-colored hair, there came to him one night a question that he had never before posed himself, one that he had, perhaps consciously, never even formulated, or, to be more precise, refused to formulate: Why did Orville, an old, gray-haired man with brown-stained teeth and yellow fingers, buy and keep every issue of *Beauty Parade?* As soon as this question "arranged" itself, let's say, in his head, his face grew hot and red. He and Orville, Orville and he and the women. The women are *theirs,* they shared them that entire summer of his sixteenth year. He and Orville.

Orville was a color lithographer and worked for the *Journal-American.*

Jackie owned a service station, Jack's Texaco. His best mechanic, Andy, had a sister who worked as a nurse's aide in the Caledonia Hospital in Brooklyn.

Linda! Louise! Candy!

Linda! Louise! Candy!

Linda! Louise! Candy!

Music! Music! Music!

Again! Again! Again!

"My devotion, dear ladies, is endless and deep as the ocean."

The black force of Eros

UT WHAT OF THE WOMEN IN *BEAUTY PARADE?*
They have been somewhat carelessly, if
rhetorically described as "big luscious
women, all rich curves and swelling flesh
pushing out of the tight, astonishingly abbreviated costumes" of a
kind that no woman, inhabitant of the mundane world, would
ever wear or even consider wearing. But the youth whose eyes
have been bedazzled by the precise and overt lewdness of these
erotic icons will not believe this. Let's say that he can't afford to
believe it, read that as you will. There, lying on the daybed in the
corner of the musty, stiflingly hot Lang porch, is the August 1944
issue, in which six of these stupendously free and arrogantly sexual women pose in quintessential lasciviousness. They are not
wholly free, though, for their status as wives, lovers, mothers,
daughters, friends, or whores, their very existence, is dependent
upon the narrative skills of the foolish adolescent boy who
drives them and himself hither and yon in his adoring imagination. His body grows hot and dry as he thinks of them, one at a

time, waiting for his attentions, in the impossible gleam of their satin, the immaculate crispness of their lace.

They are all there, Mary Marshall, Dolores Salvati, Georgene Rydstrom, Charlotte Ryan, Nancy Ippolito, Terri O'Neill: minions and bacchantes, servants of Aphrodite and Dionysos, slaves to the black force of Eros, devotees of earthy, occulted mysteries. They order that which they desire to be done to them by their acolytes, their groveling husbands and lovers and trembling fools. They are pleased to have this power, although they are not aware of its effect on the boy who, though its creator, is obedient before it. Their not knowing is very much the same as not caring, the aristocratic aloofness of the hierophants who keep secret the sacred mysteries. They will live forever, at the behest of the dark gods, their incarnations will be endless, unceasing. Mary, Dolores, Georgene, Charlotte, Nancy, Terri.

■ ■ ■

For three months of the year, Apollo left his temple at Delphi, and his place was taken by Dionysos.

It is, surely, ludicrous to think of this stupefied boy, in 1944, as venerator of the god, but in the slow, burning days of that wartime summer, he worshiped, as it was given him to worship, as best he could. It may be that the god noticed and was pleased.

Drunk, with a half-smile, his hair bound up with aromatic grasses, a "young boy loggy with vine-must." And the burning, orange-colored sky.

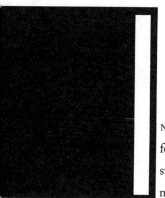

N THE STRANGELY UNBALANCED YET PER-
fect mechanics of the dream world, he's
stroking the girl's breasts through the smooth
material of a blouse or dress, while she licks a
Charlotte Russe which he holds rather carelessly. Then he's inside of
her, but with no appreciable change in their positions, and he is
mildly surprised to find that she's Ruth, after all. Her young breasts
fall easily out of her creamy-white, frothy slip. He smiles at her serious face, which seems to be receding into the suddenly dim room,
and he realizes that she doesn't know who he is. She's sweet and
kind, though, and her mouth is wet and cool and sweet, filled, as it
is, with whipped cream. He decides that he's probably going to have
an orgasm in a bed that he seems to be lying in, and as he begins to
ejaculate, she waves and walks down 14th Street, toward S. Klein's.
He wakes up, more or less, and begins to substitute for her face the
face of somebody else, he begins, that is, to arrange the dream.
Slowly, it is compromised and *written*, that is, of course, faked.

■   ■   ■

In "The Dream-Work," Freud says, quite clearly, that a dream is a picture puzzle, a rebus, and that the dream contents' hieroglyphics, or symbols, must be translated, one by one, into the language of the dream-thoughts. It is, then, incorrect to read the symbols as to their values as pictures. A rebus, that is, may not be judged as an artistic composition.

It has been smugly fashionable and acceptable for some years now to denigrate Freud as a kind of bourgeois homophobic misogynistic charlatan, wholly insensitive to the needs of This, and wholly dishonest in his writings on That. Many of those who so denigrate him have advanced degrees from excellent universities, at which latter they also teach, drive, for, doubtlessly, some intellectual reason, expensive cars, have friends with whom they—you'll pardon the expression—"play tennis"—and care not a whit for conventional thought. They are, for the most part, a credit to American education. At last count, they numbered 47,109. They dress very badly and read third-rate fiction.

In the thirties and early forties in New York, there was a Charlotte Russe "season," during which period (it was, I believe, in late spring) Charlotte Russe purveyors rented empty stores to sell their delectable confection. They remained for, perhaps, two or three weeks, then they would disappear until the following year. A mysterious hieroglyphic, or symbol. For, perhaps, the Depression.

The dreamer sometimes says, with little attention paid to accuracy, "My dreams are getting better all the time."

["Creamy-white, frothy slip" is, if you'll permit me, somewhat tired, yet I see how it "rhymes" with the Charlotte Russe motif.

"Uh-huh."]

THE OLD MAN LIGHTS A CIGARETTE AND walks into the elevator and right out its rear wall into the 69th Street ferry waiting room. He's not the man he thinks he is, though, but Buddy Mazzolini, The Boy Bus Driver, who was, at one time, the drunken cop who shot the dog on the corner outside Flynn's Bar and Grill. Somebody across the street tells him to go fuck his mother and his face turns bright blue and then black and he disappears. He drives down Ocean Parkway. Others stare at the photographs that the bus driver displays because it is quite clear that they think that these heartbreaking images will substitute for or ameliorate their ignorance. They wish the world to be kind to them, to pardon them their sins, their tattered pasts. Look at the lost people in the pictures! Look! Young, smiling, foolish, and hopeful; young, smiling, foolish, and hopeful; young, smiling, foolish, and hopeful. Sweet Mother of God!

■ ■ ■

Ghosts.

Hail, Holy Queen, Mother of mercy, our life, our sweetness, and our hope! To thee do we cry, poor banished children of Eve, to thee do we send up our sighs, mourning and weeping in this valley of tears. Turn then, most gracious advocate, thine eyes of mercy towards us; and after this our exile show unto us the blessed fruit of thy womb Jesus. O clement, O loving, O sweet Virgin Mary.

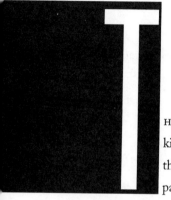

THE OLD MAN ABRUPTLY SITS DOWN ON A kitchen chair in the sunlight glaring through the window. He yields, gratefully, to the painful nausea that is attacking him and throws up black blood on his shoes and the shiny linoleum of the floor. Well, this is probably serious, he thinks. When his daughter comes into the kitchen, her face shocked pale and tight with disgust and fear, he smiles through his dirty lips, grotesquely, he knows, and prepares to tell her not to worry, she just probably has to probably call the doctor. He suspects that he, indeed, looks grotesque, smiling, but thinks that a somber face will only frighten her the more. He has the words now, and speaks them: "unspectacular explosion him, to be made smoking next, to name to name *before*." His daughter clutches one of her hands with the other, and says oh Jesus Mary and Joseph Poppa, oh Jesus Mary and Joseph. Her father waves a hand nonchalantly and adds, "overpass Luckies shoes rain of the cops, like into a gawm ticket." He pitches off the chair and lands on the floor, his face in the slick of bloody vomit. You, you, you and that goddamned rotgut whiskey, she shouts at him. She kneels and touches his hair. She was a very beautiful girl once.

■   ■   ■

To call upon Jesus, Mary, and Joseph to assist one in time of trouble was a common enough habit among many Irish Catholics in New York in the early years of the century. It may be still, but that seems doubtful.

Linoleum is now rarely used as kitchen flooring, and has, for that matter, the look of poverty, so much so that even the poor are averse to it. Oddly, its aura of poverty increases with its newness. And yet, it is not quite so louche as oilcloth, which is the absolute and incontrovertible sign of indigence, and which not even the vapid dictates of junk decoration can rescue.

That terrible events should occur on sunny, warm, and pleasant days seems a sour irony, and may well account for the quiet madness and despair, the frenzy and sudden violence, that are virtually inseparable from life in California.

Beauty is but a flowre,
Which wrinckles will devoure,
Tumbles book pencil blare,
Chow mein equities, hair . . .

TOPIAN GAMBLING SYSTEMS DEPEND ON the idea of the investment of a little money so as to make a lot of money. Such schemes are, uncharitably speaking, self-constructed cons. Of course, there are schemes that call for the investment of a lot of money to make more money, which systems work more often. These are not true, or, if you will, honest schemes, but are patterned on the loathsome practices of bankers, stockbrokers, commodities traders, venture capitalists, and other money pimps, devotees of the sure thing. Gambling, of whatever kind, is sometimes used as a metaphor for life, but that's not my fault, and it is certainly not the fault of gamblers, who never think metaphorically: a dollar is a dollar, a flush a flush, a boat race is always a boat race. Likewise, a chump is, first and foremost, a chump.

Fat Harry would take the young man to a diner on President Street and either pull out a fat sheaf of bills from a napkin that the waiter placed on the table, or put a fat sheaf of bills into a napkin, and place this at the edge of the table. In the latter case, when the waiter returned to the table with water and menus, he would pick up the cash-thick napkin, remark that it was dirty, and remove it in favor of a different napkin. When Fat Harry won, he would remark that it was a nice day, a hell of a day, and if he lost, he'd note, somberly, that the horseplayer had not been fucking born who could fucking beat the fucking nags. As he and the young man left, Fat Harry would toss a copy of the *Daily Mirror* on the counter, in whose racing pages he had marked his selections for the day. He disdained to play the horses touted by the comic strip, *Joe and Asbestos*, because of what he thought of as its ignoble practice of regularly recommending bets to place or show. This struck Harry as bush, and he would bet place and show only as part of an across-the-board wager. "You have got to have faith in the horse," Harry would say. He also told the youth that Ken Kling, the creator of the strip, was a millionaire who had *never* put a nickel on a horse. The lesson was clear.

Fat Harry, a painting foreman for Aquatic Ship Scaling, Inc., fell into the water one day at the Navy Yard, and was crushed to death between the hull of the freighter, *John H. Derrenbacher*, and the pier. A Norwegian scaler, half-drunk on his scaffold in the steamy sunlight, heard his cries and looked down to see him, thrashing in the oily water, just as the ship was heaved up on a swell and rode into the pilings. There was nothing that the scaler could do, but for a moment he thought that Harry would somehow—what?—avoid the ship? But he more or less exploded in a red surge of blood. All but one of his bets lost that day. Presidential Greetings, in the third at Santa Anita, paid 3.24 to show.

Aquatic Ship Scaling won a Navy "E" that year.

■　　■　　■

One of the napkins that occasionally turned up at the table in the diner had the letter "D" embroidered, in blue, on one of its corners. The napkin could not have represented the diner, which was named, somewhat poetically, the Rondelle.

"Maybe it stood for Dolores."

High priestess of the Navy Blue Jumper, temptress of the White Cotton Blouse, goddess of Black Lace Underwear.

While it is true that Ken Kling was a millionaire, it is also true that he played the horses, despite Fat Harry's belief. That does not mean, however, that he was a horseplayer, that is, the great steeds and contests of the royal oval did not possess him, body and soul.

[It might be worth noting that one day, Fat Harry told the young man that his youngest son, Ralphie, who was studying accounting at Fordham, was engaged to a nice girl who, Harry was pretty sure, used to live on his block. He was absurdly relieved to learn that the girl was Charlotte Ryan.]

Erratum

The hulls of ships of the considerable tonnage of the freighter, *John H. Derrenbacher,* are customarily repaired, scaled, and painted in dry dock; so that the death of Fat Harry, in the manner here described, is highly improbable.

—*Ed.*

E RINGS THE BELL AND SHE OPENS THE DOOR. This is not her family's apartment, but somebody's apartment, one of remarkably opportune availability. Somebody has gone away to Miami or someplace. Without further ado, she makes him a drink, Cutty Sark on the rocks, and they sit on the couch. She's a little drunk, or so he thinks. As soon as he kisses her, she takes off her cardigan and kisses him back. She looks curiously formal in her plain white brassiere and demure plaid skirt. There's a grand piano in the enormous living room, and it has the effect of placing him *outside* this event, if that's what it is. He touches her breasts tentatively, and she stands up and leads him into the bedroom. She sits against the headboard of the king-size bed, propped against pillows. This is the life. She tells him not to look at her, then pulls her skirt and half-slip up to her hips, and opens her thighs a little. She still has her penny loafers on. He sees that she still has her panties on, too, plain white cotton. He takes a condom, in utter despair, out of his pocket, and tears the foil wrapper open. Semper

paratus. What is he supposed to do now? He lies, awkwardly, on top of her, cradled in her arms, straddling one of her thighs, the condom between thumb and forefinger. He has no idea if he should open his pants, but he does manage to touch her crotch with the back of his hand. She says that maybe they ought to go and have coffee, Ellen will be home soon. Actually, she says that she's *afraid* that Ellen will be home soon. He doesn't know who Ellen is. Home? What about Miami? But he says, OK, sure, Ellen. What a suave customer he is. Do you want to touch me again, there, touch me there? she says. Yes, he says, blushing. He sees that she's sitting on a bath towel, another sad optimist.

■   ■   ■

"Without further ado," eh? He turns a nice phrase, useless towel and all.

The Grand Piano is yet another beautiful novel unknown to the barbarians who run things, and just as well. There are many things the existence of which should be kept hidden, lest they be soiled and cheapened.

The plaid skirt, the grand piano, the towel on the bed, etc., etc., are motifs, yes, but are they *bound* motifs?

The apartment was on Cortelyou Road.

The grand piano may figure large in subsequent tales, like a submerged bicycle, a loaded rifle on the wall, a container of yogurt. Then again, it may just be a touch of the authentic, a detail to do something or other. You know what I mean, right?

Ellen, years later, said that she entered her family's apartment at about midnight to find her friend and some "dumb-looking guy" playing Monopoly.

The girl's name was Linda, a name, incidentally, that one doesn't hear much anymore.

HE GREEK, IN HIS RENTED WHITE DINNER jacket and black tuxedo trousers, was throwing up on himself in front of the Shore Road Casino. Fat George had lost, somewhat surrealistically, half his tie and was sitting in a garbage can accompanied by a quart bottle of Rheingold, the pride of New York. Sal was attempting, in the best of humor, to persuade the short-order cook in the Royal to scramble him three eggs for the price of two, and Rocco waited outside, admiring his reflection in the plate-glass window. Nothing, but nothing, like a pearl-gray fedora! The Lion's Den was jammed with what Donnie called "revelers," and Whitey, in the spirit of revelry, was fucking Chickie in the telephone booth. In another telephone booth, a few doors away, Bromo Eddie was making random calls with the aid of a safety pin as substitute for legal tender, employing a method known and used by many citizens, though heartily condemned by Ma Bell: "It raises the costs for all, la-da, it raises the co-oosts for alll!"—of course it does! Carmine felt that Whitey shouldn't be doing what he was doing, people had to *use* that goddamn phone booth, for Christ sake. What if somebody needed an ambulance, too? Had he no home? Couldn't he fuck Chickie in the park under some bush or some damn plant? Donnie noted Carmine's objections in a spiral notebook on whose cover he had written, "Local Color." The other Sal was studying a menu in the diner, although Anna, his companion for the evening, was adamant about ordering the Cheeseburger à la Deluxe, to wit: "I am not eating any fucking soup, Sally!" Red punched Mickey just for the hell of it and then arrogantly appropriated his beer. The police were called by a citizen fed up with something or other noise or some girl who was being bothered or too loud and the neighborhood was gone to the dogs. And fuck the cops too! "Drunken boat," he said. And then again, "drunken boat." The bars closed at four, and at least thirty revelers sat in the breathless park with cardboard containers of beer until seven-thirty, then walked back to the Lion's Den and waited for the doors to open, although the joint really had but one door. "Poetic license," he said. "He who catches the early bird, catches the early bird," Donnie said. "It's the same as a drunk's coat," Fat George said. He smelled, of course, but not too badly, of garbage. Yet his chums reasoned well that a little garbage never hurt a Greek olive peddler. That was the God's honest truth, and so they swore on their mothers! Cheech and Nickie stood at the saloon door and watched the girls on their way to the subway and work, work, work! Idle pleasures, indeed. Mary passed and told Nickie that he was a bum. Dolores passed and told Cheech that he was a disgraceful bum. Georgene passed and told Nickie that he ought to be ashamed of himself, to look at himself at eight o'clock in the morning. There was no chance that *he'd* ever pass the police test! They were all impossibly beautiful in their high heels and pleated skirts. Not for the likes of "you bums," Donnie yelled from the end of the bar. Tommy Azzerini passed and told Nickie and Cheech that they talked like a coupla guys with paper assholes, although they had not addressed him. Nickie offered to knock him on his ass and Tommy said, in effect, oh, buy me a beer, for Christ sake, you guinea bastard. Pat exited his apartment building, pale, shaking, and, just an inch or so removed from a fine bout with the horrors, carefully made his way to Carroll's for a double Three Feathers and a large beer chaser; ahead lay another day of honest labor for the youthful Irish American. The salt of the earth, the coat of the drunk, the boat of the revelers, the indisposed and lazy, the insulted and injured, the hurt, the forgotten, the salt in your stew. The sail in your dreamboat. The Greek arrived, smelling of vomit, looking, as he drolly put it, for "the party." Many were called, oh many, and none were chosen. Pat sat back in the cab as it made its way to Joralemon Street and his, as he liked to put it, "place of business," and amused the cabbie mightily by unsuccessfully attempting to touch the trembling flames of many matches to his cigarette. Cabbies take their laughs where they can get them, disgraceful bums that some of them are. Others, however, are the salt of the earth, good family men, the cream in your coffee, and were or will be ready to serve their country when called. "Not as fucking asshole officers, though," Fat George opined.

■　■　■

It has never been determined why Plato Makarios Costas was in rented dinner jacket and trousers, nor what he was doing in front of the Shore Road Casino. (It is, perhaps, unnecessary to note that these garments were rented.)

This particular night and morning were rife with what neighbors called "mixed emotions." However, one of the revelers surprised most of those interviewed, since he was described by everyone as "very quiet." One man, who did not wish to give his name, revealed that "he liked to read *Sexology,* but he was real quiet."

Asked what it was like to be ogled by young, disreputable men with whom they had grown up on the mean streets, the "girls," as they insist on calling themselves, were, basically, unanimous in their replies, e.g., "the bums ought to hang their heads in shame."

Mary noted that Nickie had been an *altar boy!*

Dolores revealed that Cheech had penned a very interesting book report on *Men of Iron* by Howard Pyle.

Georgene admitted that Nickie once carried a bag of groceries home for her mother, who remarked: What A Nice Boy.

Well. Live and learn.

Where is their deep purple, their stardust, their winter wonderland and beer barrel polka and string of pearls? Where are their jingle bells and paper dolls and silent nights and glittering funny hats?

"Oh, for the love of Jesus and His Blessed Mother, give it a fucking rest, OK?"

Every fourth one on the house, and to the Republic for which it stands!

E SAYS, SO WHAT DO YOU THINK, RED? How's the fuckin' Marines treating you? He looks up, arrogantly, from the bar and the big Irish lunk swings on him and knocks him off his stool, right across the space between the bar and the booths along the wall, so that he lands on his back beneath a table, blood pouring from his broken nose and split-open lip. How I love the kisses of Dolores, he thinks, for no reason at all, and then he thinks, for the first time in years, of Dolores. When he was fifteen or sixteen, he kept her company one night when she baby-sat for a neighbor. There was a piano in the apartment, a little upright against the wall, under a pitifully inept fake oil of pinkish clouds over a white sailboat on a lake the weird blue of Aqua Velva. Dolores, frowning beautifully, began to play the piano in a dreadfully mechanical way. He smiled, since he was helplessly in love with her, and her impossibly bad performance was as nothing to her sweet, dark virginity. She banged a tinny chord and then told him that she was very sad and tired of being a good student and that she wanted to do something, something, that she wanted to do *something*. Her face was as calm and beautiful as the Virgin's. He turned this confidence into something else, sexual and forbidden. Of course.

Noise and commotion possess the bar and he decides that he'd better just lie there and stay out of the general brawl that is growing in the sickeningly inevitable way that brawls do. Barroom brawls are high-spirited affairs, with laughs and thrills, only in the movies. Who's that Norwegian jarhead, who's that punk jarhead?, lemme kick that son of a bitch's ass!, somebody shouts. Red's Irish, he says, to the bottom of the table. He's glad that Dolores, wherever she is, didn't see him get knocked flat. Fat George looks underneath the table, smiling, and holds out a bottle of beer to him. You're not gonna eat any white clam sauce with that mouth, sport, right? He sings to Fat George: How I love the kisses of Dolores, only my Dolores. Well, he's still got all his teeth.

Another night among the many that these young men in Brooklyn had *to call their own*, something, ah yes, that *nobody could take away from them*. Some think that experiences such as these build character, but they don't. But they don't. I'm enthralled, he says to Fat George, enthralled and thankful and proud to be a small part of neighborhood lore, yet again, and so will Dolores be proud, or so I have decided to pretend. Come out from under there, Fat George says, you look like shit. Dolores! Jesus.

■ ■ ■

"Dolores" was a hit song in 1941. Words by Frank Loesser, music by Louis Alter.

Dolores, at the time of the "piano incident," was, as you may know, a sophomore at Fontbonne Hall, an academically excellent and socially genteel high school for very smart Catholic girls. The girls wore navy-blue wool serge jumpers, white blouses, black ties, black knee socks or white anklets, and black shoes. Young men, seized, as they were, by Eros, often ground their teeth in hopeless desire when gazing upon the more comely of these girls. These amorous reactions were surely not intended by those who devised the puritanical uniforms. The flesh is unruly.

The various acts of violence noted here occurred in Henry's, an actual bar; "Red," however, exists only in fiction, from which, it appears, he has escaped. Or, being a Marine, from which he has apparently gone AWOL.

An AWOL bag was a soldier's term for a soft overnight or gym bag. Perhaps it still is.

A Jodie suit was, traditionally, a badly cut civilian suit of O.D. wool, given to prisoners upon their release, with Bad Conduct Discharges, from the stockade. Out into the world they went in these condemnatory rags. To make a brand-new start.

Jodie was a legendary figure who always managed to avoid military service. He was loathed and envied by the dog soldier, for his reward for shirking his duty was the easy acquisition of good jobs, plenty of money, excellent clothes, the best food and booze, and all the women he wanted. There was a shining American-ness to his exploits, for he was the man who got what he did not deserve.

EXHIBIT:

Jodie says he feels all right,
'Cause he fucked your wife last night,
Sound off! One, two,
Sound off! Three, four!
Cadence count!
One! Two! Three! Four!
One-two!
Three FOUR!

O, HERE ARE A FEW QUESTIONS FOR YOU dopes—losers all—in the candy store, or, for all I care, in a contemporary facsimile of same.

Why are not those glittering stars of the silver screen at home, fixing a tuna salad sandwich on whole wheat with lettuce and mayo, and a cold beer?

Why aren't they learning to read and write?

Is it possible that they are neglecting this golden opportunity, away from the rigors of the set, to shine their many pairs of extremely expensive shoes?

Why don't they use just a jot of the varied and profound expertise gained in preparing for their many and diverse roles—and playing them well enough to be remembered, one hopes, at "Oscar time"—to prove that the light of bowling alleys is romantic?

Don't they have anything better to do with their time than fix breakfast for the children, hurry them off to school, and then buckle down to seemingly endless domestic chores, not to mention shopping?

Why don't they trust the housekeeper or the maids or the gardeners or the chauffeurs or secretaries or valets or personal assistants, or personal trainers, tennis pros, golf pros, swimming instructors, gurus of mystical bent, and sundry astrologers and pool boys to sweep the floors, at least?

Why are they forever comfortable and really swell and relaxed in their old T-shirts and ripped, faded jeans?

Why don't they learn, for Christ's sake, to write a decent string quartet *for once?*

Why don't they find out where Parkside Avenue is? Or Ridge Crest Terrace? Or Charles Lane?

Why do they refuse to recognize that Scientology was, originally, a card game, something like Casino?

Why don't they lay off the goddamned cream of tomato soup?

Why do so many of them retreat to the sanctuary of the Zen rock garden in the Bel Air place whenever the "blow-job theory" as it pertains to inexplicable success, is mentioned?

Why don't they go home to Ashtabula?

Why, to borrow Raymond Chandler's phrase, are "all their brains in their faces"?

Why do they think that Raymond Chandler is a cocaine connection?

Why can't they spell "cocaine"?

Or, for that matter, "connection"?

Or, for that matter, "MGM"?

How come they can't shoot pool?

Why don't they like the notion of themselves as "overnight successes"?

Does it have anything to do with the "blow-job theory"?

Why don't they learn how to open clams?

Why do they hate to be recognized?

Why do they think that they "work hard" for their money?

Why do they wish they could "just walk down the street" like "anybody else"?

Why do they rarely, if ever, *really* hurt themselves on skis or in boats, planes, and cars?

Why do they seem to live on and on?

Does it have anything to do with the money that they work so terribly, terribly hard for?

Why are they always in and out of one clinic or another?

Why don't they stop throwing up on people?

Why do they think that fashion designers are artists?

Why do they think that they themselves are artists?

Why are they eternally honing their fucking craft?

Why don't they know the words to "Prisoner of Love"?

Why must they have recently learned to "appreciate" jazz?

Why can't they make a decent marinara sauce?

Why don't they stop sucking on that bottled water?

Why do they drive such dumb cars?

Why do they think that they can write?

Why do they think that they can write *poems?*

Why do they all go to the same restaurants and then go to the same restaurants and then go to the same restaurants and then go to the same new restaurant?

Why do they eat egg-white omelets?

Is it true that they will hump anything that will stand still?

Why don't they get rid of their grand pianos?

Their acoustic guitars?

Their "outsider" art?

Why are they such glorious marks for fake paintings, fake antiques, and fake first editions?

Should they drop dead already *en masse,* or one at a time?

■　■　■

Belatedly, Bromo Eddie queries: "Why don't they go fuck themselves?" What a serious and well-informed citizen and consumer Eddie is!

What, precisely, is the "blow-job theory" of inexplicable success, and is it germane to occupations other than the movie business?

Eddie reminds his chums that he prefers the term "film business."

Did many of these basically regular folks have gals and fellas back home in, say, ah, Moline?

What is the joke which bears this punch line? "Well, how about ten dollars' worth?"

Can one actually "fix" a cold beer?

E ENTERS THE RESTAURANT WITH HIS
mother, into the wonderful smell of the bar,
just opened on Sunday early afternoon, the
serious, adult smell of whiskey and bitters,
lemon peel, gin and vermouth and rum; the sweet and sharp cigarette smoke from the first patrons, sitting quietly with their
griefs and their hangovers and their Sunday papers, waiting
patiently for the liquor to make the slow afternoon sadly bearable.
He orders a Gibson, his mother a Clover Club, or is it a Jack Rose?
He waits for her comments on his news, given her, abruptly, two
days earlier, regarding his plans to marry, suddenly, a girl whom his
mother dislikes a good deal. Not only is she a Protestant, but she
is much too young, not even out of high school, so his mother
insists despite the facts. The cocktails arrive, his mother takes out
a pack of Herbert Tareytons and lights one with her beautiful little jewel of a Dunhill lighter, inhales and blows smoke at an angle
past the little brim of her small black velvet hat. She is an attractive woman, whose terror and loathing of men has been elegantly

metamorphosed, over the years, into an aloof but sharp contempt. She puts the lighter squarely on top of the cigarette pack. So, she says. Have you given any thought to this, you lummox? He looks at her and shrugs, a gesture of love, intimacy, and respect. The trouble with this girl, she says, that is, one of the troubles that I can see, is. She stops, and takes a sip of her gorgeously blushing cocktail. Is, she says, simply that she is obviously a little tramp. Do you, dear God, want *another* little tramp to set next to the first one? At least she was Jewish.

■　■　■

The restaurant was on Montague Street in Brooklyn Heights. It may well have been Armando's. It looks like Armando's.

The young man once accidentally saw his mother, through a half-open door, as she was dressing, and spied on her, shamed and disturbed. He has trained himself, if "trained" is the word, to think of her, on that particular day, as a woman wholly different from the woman he sits across from in the restaurant. In this way, even a hint, a breath of the incestuous may be successfully proscribed. More or less.

The Gibson was made with Beefeater gin, one of the small glories of this humdrum life.

CLOVER CLUB

Juice 1/2 Lemon.

2 Tsps. Grenadine.

White of 1 Egg.

1 1/2 oz. Dry Gin.

Shake well with cracked ice and strain into a 4 oz. cocktail glass.

JACK ROSE

1 1/2 oz. Applejack.

Juice 1/2 Lime.

1 tsp. Grenadine.

Shake well with cracked ice and strain into a 3 oz. cocktail glass.

HE CLIPPER, BOWLING THROUGH HEAVY glassy seas, all sails set, straining and singing in the wind, holds still, as always and ever, on the side of the laminated cardboard wastebasket. Just as still as the clipper is the woman, paralyzed drunk, athwart the hotel room bed. She is in her mid-fifties, and her face is attractive, though her blond hair is clearly too yellow to be natural. Her skirt, which has ridden up revealingly but not quite immodestly to mid-thigh, allows her legs to be seen as strong, straight, and well-made, with generous thighs, superbly shaped calves, and slender ankles. She is wearing a hat, cone-shaped, of shiny purple paper, which declares, in a sadly blatant red, HAPPY NEW YEAR. The hat is askew, and she snores, quietly, her mouth open. The young man, sitting at the little secretary on a hard straight chair in dim lamplight, finishes the whiskey in a thick bathroom glass, pours the last of a fifth of Ballantine's scotch into it, and drinks that too.

He'll maybe put her to bed, but he won't, God, undress her. He is upset because he has allowed himself to think that she has very good legs. Maybe he'll just put a blanket over her. Maybe he'll go get another bottle, maybe he'll leave and go to one of the bleakly frenzied parties he's been invited to, or go to a crazed bar, or go for a walk, or go get laid. Maybe he'll jump off the fucking pier or in front of the Fourth Avenue Local. Maybe he'll just sit there until she wakes up and then ask her who she thinks she is, who she thinks he is to say what she said to him, and then to say it again. Love? she said, love? For Christ's sweet sake, don't make me laugh, I'm the one who said she was nothing but a tramp. Now you're surprised?

Somebody on that clipper ship is probably looking at him from its shuddering deck, yo-ho! He knows this to be a fact, oh Christ, yes, he knows many things, he does, except why he's here with his drunken mother in dark and sleety Brooklyn, in the dark and iron world.

■ ■ ■

There has been a great deal written on clipper ships, and "the Age" of the clipper ship, none of which information is of any interest to this young man.

At the time of this particular New Year's Eve, disco had not yet been invented. One less thing for white, middle-class, suburban heroes of irony to mock.

Speaking of hotels: The chances that a meat-cutting-machine salesman, let's call him Lester Peck, in, say, a Binghamton cocktail lounge, might strike up a conversation with a comely middle-aged businesswoman, take her to his room in the local Sheraton, and there discover her to be wearing nothing beneath her tailored business suit, are so small as to be virtually nonexistent. As we speak, there sits Lester, at the Sheraton bar, talking man-talk with the bartender about, oh yes!, the heroic NFL.

It's love, love, love, all right, but not for lonely Lester, the football enthusiast.

That the woman lying athwart the hotel bed is a bleached blonde is, all right, a cliché of sorts, but what is one to do?

What One Is To Do: ". . . her face is attractive, though her hair is gray"; ". . . her face is attractive, though her hair needs a shampoo"; ". . . her face is attractive, though she is no longer the crack sales representative for Pfister & Sons Restaurant Products, Inc., that she once was."

"Bright Night, I obey thee, and am come at thy call."

Come, though, to what?

HEN HIS MOTHER DIED, HE WAS CIVIL, even somewhat friendly toward the handsome and correctly serious priest who had come to the hospital to administer extreme unction, which sacrament, he learned, was now called "anointing of the sick." He was grateful, in his apostate's ignorance, to be so enlightened. He had, after all, won, at the age of twelve, a certificate for Excellence in Religious Studies, signed by Monsignor Patrick J. O'Hara.

She was waked out of the same funeral home that had waked his grandmother, grandfather, and aunt. The mother of his closest boyhood friend came on the second night of the wake, embraced him, then knelt at the casket and wept more bitterly than he thought it possible for anyone to weep. He realized, not for the first time, that his mother had lived a life of her own, a life other than the one he recognized, a life wholly hidden from him, but known to others. He arranged for a High Requiem mass, and she was buried next to her mother in Holy Cross cemetery. He ordered a stone for her from Iavoni and Sons, to carry her name and dates of birth and death. After the stone had been finished and put in place, he learned that she was four years older than she had always claimed. Well, she had been a vain woman, proud of her looks and figure, meticulous in her dress, stiffnecked and vindictive yet "full of fun," as she might say, and oddly puritanical and bawdy at once. She was perfectly willing to terminate friendships of years' standing in an instant, and her overt sentimentalism was but a mask for her absolute toughness and contempt for most of the people she had to do with. She would have liked the mass, the black-and-silver vestments, the properly gloomy church, the singing and the candles: the works. That's what she'd wanted, that's what she got.

A month or so later, he went to the parish church she'd been buried out of and lighted a candle for her, but said no prayers. He sat in a pew, inhaling the coolly thin odor of wax and lingering incense in the air. He had spent years and years going to mass in this church, wherein he had been baptized, received his First Holy Communion, been confirmed. That he'd done his duty by his mother, relied on the church as she would have wanted him to, made him feel himself more remote than ever from this complex religion, more excluded from its enigmas and paradoxes. The abyss is just that, so he thought, and his mother was nowhere at all, gone, gone into the gloom of oblivion. He walked out into the familiar streets on which he had grown up into doubt and weakness and error. World without end? Shuffle off to Buffalo.

■   ■   ■

When all is said and done—lovely phrase—it has to be acknowledged that Roman Catholicism is not a Christian religion; or, to put it better, the neurotically cheerful, doom-obsessed, you-can-take-it-with-you hysteria of eccentric American Christianity has little to do with Roman Catholicism, which is, essentially, a mystery religion. All those worldly priests who can chat about mundane problems are but masks and diversions to hide the center of the faith from the general, snarling populace, lest they should see it for what it is: magic.

The woman who wept herself into hysteria was Katie DeLeon. Two other women, who also wept so uncontrollably that they had to be helped out of the viewing room, were Anna Claves and Mary Filippo. He sat with each of them, individually, on a small love seat outside of the funeral director's office, and each gripped his hand and held white handkerchiefs, sodden with tears, to their streaming, swollen eyes. The handkerchiefs had lace edgings.

"Anointing of the sick" has a more hopeful sound to it than "extreme unction." As if "the sick" may perhaps recover.

"Shuffle Off to Buffalo" was published in 1932, words by Al Dubin, music by the wondrous Harry Warren. Ginger Rogers and Ruby Keeler sang this song, and, of course, danced to it, on a Hollywood back-lot version of the Niagara Limited. The film was *Forty-Second Street.*

Al Dubin, Harry Warren, Ruby Keeler, Ginger Rogers, and the Niagara Limited are all dead. Let perpetual light shine upon them.

HE DAY HIS MOTHER DIED WAS A COLD DAY. The day his mother died was a wet day. The day his mother died was a raw day, a snowy day. The day his mother died was a gray day, the gray of death.

The day his mother died was a dark day, a day of cheap chow mein, of Lucky Strikes, of somber faces, of silent relatives, of soothing clichés, a day of sadness.

The day his mother died was a day of revelations, bitterness, a day of sudden understanding, of ignorance, of mysteries and confessions, of trips and trips and trips through sleet and freezing rain in cars and cabs and subway trains, in the Hudson Tubes, in Public Service buses, on foot through slushy streets.

The day his mother died ended some things and initiated others.

The day his mother died was a day of memories, of old movies, of yellowing books and brittle pages and of bad poems, blurry television screens, of new kitchenware, of policemen and doctors and oxygen and anesthesia, of stupid articles and vapid stories in tattered magazines.

The day his mother died was a day of copulation, fellatio, masturbation, cunnilingus, it was a day of girdles and hats with half-veils, of high heels and dinner rings.

The day his mother died was a day of insanity and hamburgers, of perversions, of good clothes and fur coats and bank accounts, of booze and quiet saloons, of surrogate court and legal forms and leaky ballpoint pens.

A day of undertakers and morgues, of helplessness, of sheer stockings, dresses cut on the bias, lipstick, perfume, mascara, eye shadow, of rouge and neckties and embarrassment. Of formaldehyde.

A day of children in patched clothes, windy empty lots, bad jobs, pitiful salaries, cruel and stupid bosses, of rickety furniture and basement apartments, of drunkenness and false friends, of hopeless misunderstandings. It was a day of coarse and vulgar infidelities, instant violence, reckless fucking, crazed parties, insincere smiles, of error and sin and betrayal. It was a day of unwanted confidences and cynicism.

The day his mother died: of death: a day of negation: of finality.

Mourning and weeping. In this valley of tears.

■   ■   ■

"The phrase, 'the day his mother died,' has an intentionally incantatory quality, of course, but may it not be considered self-indulgent?"

Death strolls down the road and asks if we might care to sit in the shade of a tree with him. An old elm, what else? A cool breeze blows across the overgrown churchyard and the old church is piercingly white in the bright sun. "Smoke 'em if you got 'em," he says.

He seems like a reasonable man, for a corporal. Of course, he's got a job to do.

It is very difficult for a young man to select the clothes that his mother will be buried in. Let the women do it, for Christ's sake, let the women do it.

He sits in the dim light of the shabby living room, watching the snow pile up against the badly seated windows. "I really *liked* her," the woman says. "God, she was just here a month ago." A marvel, a masterpiece, a chef d'oeuvre of cant.

He sees *her* clearly, 'deed he do. "That's a fucking jewel of fucking phoniness," he says. "Do we have any whiskey in this fucking hateful dump?"

A day of bad movies, of the silver screen filled with the paralyzing stupidity of self-adoration. "These swine will never die!"

Snow snow. Snow.

She whom no one ever found, death found, in Jersey City.

SHE TOLD HIM THAT HIS FATHER WAS THE greatest driver in the country, if not the world, and that LaSalles and Packards, DeSotos and Chryslers, Buicks and Cadillacs and Hudson Terraplanes had been designed and built especially for his pleasure; that he had suggested the wooden-spoked wheels for the Moon roadster and sold the specifications for another famous if overrated car to Herr Porsche, who then claimed it for his own; that dances had been created for him by Nijinsky, Ted Shawn, Isadora Duncan, Martha Graham, and Loie Fuller, that ballrooms had been named for him and luncheon dances under swirling colored lights suggested and popularized by him. The classic Savile Row suit? Designed by him. The Windsor knot? First tied by him and generously credited to the Duke, who, in actual fact, being something, he'd winked, of "a dim bulb," couldn't even tie his shoes. The silk scarf employed as a belt was one of his improvisatory whims. He had started all the major Hollywood studios, with Jack and Adolph and Harry and Louis as his assistants, but tired of their puerile minds, their lack of adventurous spirit, and their worship of the box office. She said that he'd opened a restaurant with Rudolph Valentino as a partner; that he'd been the first to wear a midnight-blue tuxedo; that before his arrival in Miami Beach, Lincoln and Collins Avenues had been not much more than skid rows; that he'd created whipped cream and the cheeseburger; that he'd not only bought, refurbished, and opened the Cotton Club, but that he'd booked into it Duke Ellington, Billie Holiday, Chick Webb, Sy Oliver, Benny Moten, Jay McShann, Fletcher Henderson, Jimmy Lunceford, Cab Calloway, and Andy Kirk and his Twelve Clouds of Joy; that he'd collaborated with Flo Ziegfeld on all the Follies, but grew restive at the successful but banal formula, and that, incidentally, he'd made love to each and every one of the famed Ziegfeld Girls; that he'd also had affairs with Pola Negri, Clara Bow, Gloria Swanson, Mae Marsh, Vilma Banky, Paulette Goddard, Claudette Colbert, Dorothy Day, Lydia E. Pinkham, and Castoria Fletcher, all this before, *of course,* he'd met her; that he'd bought a Chinese restaurant, the Jade Mountain, with cash, because she liked the egg foo yung there, a dish, by the way, that he'd created of necessity on a chicken farm in the Gobi; that he'd almost managed to save Bix Beiderbecke from drinking himself to death, but was too busy advising the Army Air Corps on the design of a low-altitude fighter that eventually became the P-51 Mustang; that he'd caught the biggest sailfish, tuna, swordfish, and blue marlin that had ever been caught off the Florida Keys; that he'd advised James Joyce to drop the possessive apostrophe in the title of his last work; that he'd suggested to Scott

Fitzgerald that he read the work of the virtually unknown Ernest Hemingway. He invented the pneumatic scaling tool and devised a method of cleaning double-bottomed boilers that would save workers' sanity; he consistently bid lowest on re-rigging jobs for the Navy and just as consistently did excellent work; he could shovel snow for hours and then dance all night; make a marinara sauce and a bolognese sauce and a white-clam sauce that were miracles of superb flavor and subtle balance; he could teach anybody to drive and had, as a matter of fact, given the great Nuvolari some invaluable tips. She remarked that it was well known that he was a descendant of an aristocratic Italian family, descended from the Emperor Galerius, whose roots were deep in Sicily; that he was a remarkably attentive, adoring, dutiful yet strict father; that he had renamed Yellow Hook, Bay Ridge, for which the Brooklyn Borough President gave him the key to the borough and the Order of Chevalier of Kings County Arts and Letters; that he'd been the one to first spot George Herriman's genius; that he'd suggested to Magritte that the title of a simple painting should be "Ceci n'est pas une pipe," rather than the painter's "Une pipe"; that he could sing like Russ Columbo, only with greater range and better breath control; that he met regularly with Aaron Copland, Charles Ives, George Gershwin, Erik Satie, Alban Berg, and Arnold Schoenberg to discuss what he called "serial music" and "atonal music"; that he wrote the first lengthy critique of the new medium of television, calling it "the coming boon—or curse—of the century." He had unofficially broken the world records for the giant slalom, the butterfly, the 100-meter dash, and the pole vault; he advised his close friends to buy up all the cheap land in and around a small, virtually abandoned one-time mining town in Colorado: Aspen; and he was the writer or co-writer of speeches given by Franklin D. Roosevelt, Father Divine, Al Smith, Fiorello H. LaGuardia, Huey Long, Eddie Cantor, Father Coughlin, Eugene V. Debs, and General Douglas MacArthur, the latter's remarks those famous words delivered on the occasion of his being awarded his ninth Good Conduct Medal; he had, uncannily, predicted the popular musical expression that came to be called rock and roll. His heart had stopped beating for forty-seven minutes when his mother died, and he remarked, upon regaining life-functions, that "the other side" looked "like an enchanted Elizabeth Street"; he wrote all the jokes and comedy routines for W.C. Fields, Eddie Cantor, George Jessel, Milton Berle, Henny Youngman, and the Marx Brothers; he was, perhaps, proudest of the humble sausage recipe that he gave, gratis, to Nathan Handwerker; and she said, too, that he was a lying, cheating, unfaithful, deceitful, and miserably cruel and thoughtless and selfish son of a fucking bitch bastard who should suffer and suffer for years and years and then die in agony and all alone and burn screaming in the torments of hell forever and ever and ever, may God forgive me! That's what she told him.

■   ■   ■

This is, without a doubt, faintly absurd, but one may read it with Beckett in mind, who remarks that one may "puzzle over it endlessly without the least risk. For to know nothing is nothing, not to want to know anything likewise, but to be beyond knowing anything, to know you are beyond knowing anything, that is when peace enters in, to the soul of the incurious seeker. It is then that the true division begins, of twenty-two by seven, for example, and the pages fill with the true ciphers at last."

Samuel Beckett, it may be recalled, was awarded the Nobel Prize for Literature. So were many, many other people.

This woman, vexed and exasperated by life, is, in effect, saying, "I won't cry anymore, and I wish you were here," or "I wish you were here, but I won't cry anymore."

"Maybe, I mean just maybe, she's really saying, 'Come to the Mardi Gras!'"

Oh, for Christ's sweet sake, don't be so literary.

Speaking of literary, a list of selected, judiciously selected, Nobel Prize laureates in Literature, might be thought of as "the true ciphers at last."

Four soldiers

E WAS ONE OF FOUR SOLDIERS IN A SALOON
somewhere, after so many years, it's hard to
remember. That's what he says, in any event,
probably a dodge. The others cannot be
located, or accounted for, or so he says. A saloon in maybe
Baltimore, or Blackstone, maybe Glen Burnie or San Antonio.
This was another world, existent before probably three-quarters
of the people presently dwelling, as best they can upon this earth,
were born. There was a dance floor, big enough for three couples,
just off the end of the long bar and near the two booths at the
back of the room. The usual jukebox, some of the songs that year
were "And So to Sleep Again," "I Won't Cry Anymore," "Mixed
Emotions," and "Unforgettable," the last cited the only one to
have survived. A blonde. A pale-blue dress. Reminiscent of something that he could not quite place, but it may well have been
important. He was giving this blonde some story about being
shipped out in a week to FECOM, la-la, la-la, la-la. Then the
pale-blue dress presented him with another image of another girl

at another bar, OK, FECOM, oh yeah. The dress might have been a uniform, white, or an elegant sweater with tiny faux pearls in a fleur-de-lis pattern on the bosom. The feel of ice-cold fur with a hint of clean, fresh perfume.

Now, how to get this blond girl with her small breasts and lovely hips away from the other girls and his three pals, Privates E-2 Blank, Blank, and Blank? She was a little drunk and he was telling her a lot of lies, and her pale-blue dress was somehow responsible for the smell of ether and hospital meat loaf and cold, soggy carrots and peas. What the hell?

Yeah, they'll be cutting our orders for Fort Ord in a couple of days, damn it. What a sorry-looking soldier he was, his khakis disgracefully wrinkled and stained with beer and whiskey and ketchup, his low-quarters scuffed, his brass dull, his tie missing, his cap in his back pocket. He looked at her, his face suitably and bravely stricken. Honor first, yet—apprehension. And love! Love! He slid his dirty hand down the smooth fabric of her dress till it rested between the small of her back and her buttocks, and she tentatively pushed her thighs against him. But where could they go, for God's sake? A walk, a cup of coffee, a movie, bowling? Then, maybe, maybe what?

They might well have been in Wilmington, Delaware, for that matter. How come you didn't join the Navy if you, gee, don't like the Army? He told her, in hesitant speech, of his noble brother, nobly killed in action aboard the U.S.S. *Portland* in the Coral Sea, and how he'd promised their mother—an invalid now—that he'd never, never . . . oh, he told her many things, many ingenious lovely things. He had his hand on her thigh and could feel, through her skirt, where her garter clasped her stocking.

He did not tell her that he didn't mind the Army at all, that it was a place wherein you were safe in your *head*, but he dutifully pushed his groin against her belly, and she smiled at him, the lights from the jukebox flashing off the lenses of her glasses. Ah, how nice it would be to fuck her, all of her, her dress, her hair, her garters, and her glasses. She said that she really had to be getting home for supper, it was really getting late. Ah, he said. OK.

■ ■ ■

Soldiers often attempt to seduce women with announcements of their imminent dispatch into the Jaws of Death. It is an old and respected con, wholly understood by both soldiers and women.

WELCOME. MEDICAL REPLACEMENT TRAINING CENTER 2ND ARMY. FORT MEADE, MARYLAND.

One of the soldiers in the saloon on that late September afternoon had his face and both arms blown off while in action with the 5th RCT on Hill 923, somewhere near Obong-ni Ridge, North Korea; another died of multiple myeloma, as a result of exposure to radiation during a nuclear exercise in White Sands, New Mexico, where he was sent, with other troops of the 2nd Army, to serve as part of a ground-forces reaction operation; the third returned to Germany, where he had been born to parents who were soon burned to crisps in an American incendiary raid in 1944; and our man, "the dancer," after a short and unremarkable military career as a medical-aid man, moved to California, where he immediately felt, as an absolute stranger among strangers who are themselves absolute strangers among strangers, in a state not meant for human habitation, at home. One day, he saw a Jodie suit, in faded blue denim, in the window of a hip men's boutique in San Francisco.

What about the girl in the blue dress? What was her name?

The Military Occupational Specialty (MOS) designation for Medical Aid Man is 3666. During the Korean War, their mortality rate was just slightly lower that that of second lieutenants of infantry.

 E LOOKS THROUGH THE WINDOW OF THE
ground-floor sublet that she's living in for
the year. Bitter cold winds, edged and violent, crash down the street from the river.
Inside, warm lights, she's in a pale-blue knitted dress that shows
her figure in softened detail. His head is partly under her skirt, his
hands hold her upper thighs, she leans against a dresser and opens
her legs. Flurries against the streetlamps. He opens the gate onto
the small area before the apartment door, she's in a pale-blue knitted dress in the warm room, he puts his hands on her waist, she
leans against him, ah, she says. Your mouth, he says.

The martinis are blue, and so they should be, blue ruin.
They're in a bar that they like, but that nobody else does. Outside,
cold, wet flowers are bright and glistening in the florist's flat
lights. He puts his hand under the table and touches her thigh,
her dark eyes are glazed with gin and lust, she half-smiles.

He knocks at the door, and she opens it to the sublet, her
pale-blue dress in the orange light from the shaded lamp is

arresting and also familiar, a kind of blurred and shifting image, piquant. Piquant? What did you say? she says.

I'm not drunk yet, she says, and lights a cigarette. She puts her little jewel of a Dunhill lighter squarely on top of the cigarette pack. He doesn't really remember when he first saw her, or where, but he remembers that it was sweet, sweet and what else? It was piquant, she says, you are hopeless! Pale-blue dress, her sweet warm flesh stretching the fabric, blue ruin. Men turn to look at her, secretly, offhandedly, as if trying to recall something forgotten, or they look at her and then try not to look at her: What's the use? She crosses her legs and pulls the hem of her skirt down deftly. He lights her cigarette. Looking in your eyes is like looking at your you-know, he says. How dirty and filthy you are, she says, and *now* I'm drunk. The snow begins, slight, dusty, whispery, and the wind dies.

He knocks at the door and she opens it, her pale-blue knitted dress comes to mid-knee, nice dress, he says, I think I'm going to have to look right under it. I thought you had that filthy perverted gleam in your eye, she says. He wants her to take the dress off and leave it on, he wants her to be naked and half-naked, he wants, he wants, he wants. This is a really nice apartment, he says, and pretends to look carefully around. Come on and fuck me, she says, pulling her dress off over her head. What kind of a boyfriend are *you?*

They have a fourth martini, what the hell. Look at the snow, she says, I think we better get drunk. And go to a drunk bar, he says, a drunker bar, you know. The bartender looks at her breasts move under the knitted fabric. The place has the soft, warm glow of hope, faint hope, to be sure, but hope nonetheless. Or we can go to my place, she says, my beautiful furnished sublet, conveniently located near subway and bus stops, where you can do things to me all night long, even though you don't really love me or even care? She's right, but he smiles.

■　■　■

The pale-blue dress into which this young woman—let's call her Margie—has been placed, probably against her better judgment, somehow reminds a musician, trudging through the snow past Margie's ground-floor apartment, of Sonny Rollins's supreme "Blue Seven," which, or so the musician notes, "derives much of its uncanny beauty through the use of the Lydian scale."

"And the Lydian scale has to do with Margie's dress . . . how?"

The reader is always in my thoughts, especially when she is in the Lydian mode, which is often blue, as in knitted dress.

Oh clement, oh loving, oh sweet!

SHE TURNS AWAY FROM THE WINDOW THAT looks over the courtyard into which snow, the first storm of the winter, is heavily falling, then smiles at him and pulls her slip off over her head. He's pleased to see that she's wearing white under-clothes. This would seem to be or perhaps he'd like it to be the late afternoon or early evening of their wedding day. They are well-fed and slightly drunk. There's a bottle of Sauvignon Blanc in the small, frost-choked refrigerator and a half-quart of vodka in the cupboard. Plenty of cigarettes. Hotcha! She keeps her lingerie in an old metal breadbox, white with a motif of tiny yellow flowers, that she bought for a dime at a sidewalk sale outside the dairy-and-egg store. She walks to the window and looks at the snow falling heavily in the courtyard and he looks at her body and smiles. They've been in this apartment for six months, and some of their books and records and clothes and dishes have not yet been unpacked, a bad sign, perhaps, if you believe in signs. She walks toward the bathroom, her slip immaculately flowing, that's the word, from her hand. What whiteness will you add to this whiteness, what candor? "What whiteness will you add to this whiteness, what candor?" he says, and she looks over her shoulder at him and shakes her white slip. He sits on the couch, waiting for her to finish her shower, drinking Scotch and smoking. There's plenty of Scotch left. Once, she threw what he remembers as a pale-blue dress on the battered studio couch and pulled her slip off over her head in a perfect sexual silence. He'd never seen her even partially undressed, and now, here she was. The radio was playing softly, some WBAI Mozart chestnut, the January wind battering the drafty old frame house. She opened the lingerie box and removed white things: soft luster, lace. He sat back and watched her. Wedding bells are breaking up that old gang of mine, and so? He touched a small, pale scar on his thigh, a souvenir of a scratch her cat had given him the first night they'd slept together. Some years before, he'd had a dream in which he'd pushed a woman out of the bed and she fell on the floor, her nightgown up around her waist. "What a fucking jerk," the woman laughed, "I might have known." One of the cartons had the letter "K" for "kitchen" on its side, or for "strikeout." "Strikeout?" she'd said. When he went out to buy cigarettes and cash his ridiculous paycheck he expected her to be asleep when he returned, but she was ironing his shirts in black cotton underpants and a torn Sarah Lawrence T-shirt. She had his worn rubber zoris on. He held up the two bottles of cheap Bordeaux he'd also bought, and she lifted the iron in a toast to penury. He would have preferred it had she been wearing the pale-blue dress that she'd worn the night they first made love in his new apartment. Or was that another night? Or was it a pale-blue blouse or slip? It's draped carelessly over the back of a kitchen chair, and she reaches for it and says that she had better get home before the shabby cheap son of a bitch who shares the rent with her steals her television set. They spent most of the early morning lying on the couch in somebody else's apartment, listening to unfamiliar records. "One of these days I'll get a place," he says. "Uh-huh," she says. The snow falls at a sharp angle past the window and into the early morning silence of Avenue A. She keeps a change of clothes in a plastic Key Food bag. After they dress, he looks at his watch and discovers that it's only 8:30. For some reason, this day reminds him of their wedding day. He is pleased that she's wearing a white brassiere, and he tells her so. Actually, he says, "Hotcha! Wotta pair!" and leers at her. She's irritated and hurt by this and they begin to quarrel and she packs her few things together and leaves. He watches her walk across the snowy park and then he opens the window and throws his wristwatch out onto the avenue, the fucking idiot. He poured her a glass of cheap Bordeaux and they ate Chinese food, smiling at each other in the new daze of new love. When he came back with the wine she was wearing white ankle-strap heels, the very shoes she'd worn the day they got married. "Aha, fuck-me shoes, she hinted," he said. She hit him with a pillow on which was embroidered *Handsome Is As Handsome Does.* She sat across from him in the early September light that touched her sweet, sad face, and he began to laugh from sheerest love, O love. She sits back in the bleached-out Adirondack chair in a white T-shirt and pleated white shorts, her feet bare, and he gets up and kneels in front of her and puts his face between her thighs. She strokes his hair, soon they'll be married, or so he thinks. He says something about it. He lifted his head to see her looking at the snow falling past the window. She stands up, her warm thighs touch his upturned face, and she pulls her white slip off over her head. She is wearing white underclothes. He watches her take a breadbox down from a closet shelf. A breadbox? He hasn't seen a breadbox since the Depression. This was the early evening of their wedding day? Maybe. She lights a cigarette and puts the pack down on top of her pale-blue dress, thrown carelessly on the bookcase. "So what are your lewd plans for me this evening, you dirty filthy thing?" she says. O gay sweet careless love.

■   ■   ■

The congruences of life are as relentless as they are poignant. Love, O love, O careless love.

"That this man, or one of them, is pleased that this woman, or one of them, is wearing white underclothes, would seem to strongly suggest that he is easily pleased."

I was under the impression that we were more or less done with that pale-blue dress. Not that I mind!

"A man delighted with his beloved's dress is a man who is, one might argue, easily delighted."

Is this woman, or women, or whatever the hell is going on here, Dolores?

"Dolores asserts herself again in this memoir, although I use the word 'memoir' as a figure of speech, of course."

"Memoir" or not, Dolores and her lady friends are heartbreakers all.

Harke, all you ladies that do sleep:
    the fayry queen Proserpina
Bids you awake and pitie them that weepe;
    you may doe in the darke

What the day doth forbid:

    feare not the dogs that barke,

        Night will have all hid.

"With the golden crown, Aphrodite,

Cypri munimenta sortita est."

"Thou with dark eyelids."

SHE IS ON HER KNEES, NEXT TO THE Christmas tree, her forearms on the edge of the worn couch. Her posture is reverential, even pious, although her skirt is up around her waist and her panties are down to the middle of her thighs, so that her buttocks are invitingly prominent between the torn white-lace trim of her slip and the dark tops of her stockings. He fucks her slowly and with fixed determination, by the living Christ he'll prove to her that she loves him, no matter what she thinks she feels. He knows, though, that she doesn't love him anymore, which is why he is fucking her so seriously. It would be nice if there were some goddamn heat in the dump of an apartment! He hates his stupid life, and hates hers even more. But he'll show the bitch what a real fuck is. It is an intensely and violently erotic moment.

■ ■ ■

The couple so flagrantly and vulgarly spied upon for the voyeuristic pleasure of the reader (who is always in my thoughts) has been married for almost eleven years.

The magnificent "Blue Seven," by Sonny Rollins, is playing on the phonograph during what I think should be called—and why not?—this "erotic moment."

The Christmas tree! It could well have become, had this erotic moment been turned into a story, an image, crisp with irony, yet poignant with shared memory. Perhaps the reader once engaged in lovemaking under or next to a Christmas tree, and so can relate, and relate well, to the truth of the scene.

There are very few stories that we have not heard, popular opinion notwithstanding, very few indeed.

Writing, such as it is, that doesn't quite become story, is often described, even condemned, as self-indulgent. And so it is. And no! The meaning of "such as it is" is not clear. It seems, somehow, crisp with irony.

The reader is always in my thoughts, as I think I've admitted.

HEY REMEMBERED, FOR YEARS, THE BAR-
becue they went to in East Orange, in
somebody's car. It was a lovely 4th of July,
cool and sunny and dry, with a steady, fresh
breeze off the Atlantic. In any event, that's where death began
or, perhaps, asserted itself. When questioned about it a few
months later, everyone agreed, separately, that it began to
become clear somewhere toward late afternoon, just before they
got back in the car to return to the city. It wasn't the day itself,
certainly. The day was relaxed and cheerful, there were people
everywhere, music and dancing, and no one got terribly drunk.
A lot of people brought their children, as a matter of fact. It
seemed to be the sort of 4th of July that is proffered as the
American small-town norm, celebrant with bands and parades
and picnics on the town mall or under the trees next to the
Grange Hall. And yet there is no denying the fact that something happened, ribs, hot dogs, hamburgers, corn on the cob,
kegs of beer, and the Stars and Stripes notwithstanding. Not

even "The Washington Post March" could have overwhelmed it. There is a photograph to prove it.

■   ■   ■

Darkness and oblivion are often recognized by means of the small, tentative steps taken toward the "realm of silence," and at the most unlikely times in the most unlikely places.

The driver of the car reportedly cried out, spitting out partly chewed kernels of sweet (butter-and-cream) corn, "Angels and ministers of grace defend us!" This should count as a rumor. Many years later, on his deathbed, he said, "Five minutes more?" as if his nurse could grant this request.

A regiment, its battalions under their snapping flags and guidons, wheeling, company by company, at the far end of a parade grounds so as to pass in review, often marches to John Philip Sousa, the "semper fidelis maniac," as Edward Dorn calls him in one of the great poems of the century. Such a regiment on parade is something to see.

Incidentally, "Five minutes more?" is, essentially, what Dr. Faustus cried out when his time came.

John Philip Sousa knew all of *Hamlet* and *Dr. Faustus* by heart. Or so the driver of the car said.

E MORE OR LESS INTENDED TO MAKE A fool of himself. That's what he wanted to do, wanted to be, a fool. He got drunk in a rather casual way, not so as to be able to make a fool of himself, but so as to be able to deny to himself that he wanted to do this. A subtle drunk, oh yes, and a subtle fool. It might be useful to remember that the woman he called up was a woman he hadn't seen in many years. He had, as the serviceable locution puts it, gotten over her almost immediately after she had broken off their relationship, or whatever she called it. Relationship sounds like her kind of word. He had, as a matter of fact, not even thought of her for eleven years, and here he was, in a saloon's phone booth, calling her up. People are, for the most part, utterly absurd. This is proven over and over again.

After she realized who it was on the line, she expressed a kind of bored surprise, then an equally bored irritation, and then he confessed, lying wildly, in a kind of gallant improvisation, that he still loved her, he had always and always loved her, he was crazy about her still, he thought of her constantly. He had, he said, built a sort of a shrine to her in his memory. That's what he said. Oh, brother!

Her husband got on the line then and shouted at him and he surprised himself by suddenly sobbing. He hung up, got out of the booth, and sat at the bar. He'd be late for supper again, and when he got home his wife would be angry and silent and the food would be in the refrigerator already. Why go home? Maybe there was somebody else he could call. He used to know a lot of girls. How about Amelia, in the black dress, he knew her! And then there were all the other ones, the other girls he knew once.

The bartender dropped a coaster in front of him and he ordered a Fleischmann's with beer back. The bartender paid no attention to the fact that he was still sniffling. I made some goddamn fool of myself, he said to the bartender, some goddamn fool! He banged his fist on the bar. The bartender poured a hooker of whiskey and drew a beer. You're not gonna give me any grief, are you, champ? He shook his head. No grief, he said. He threw the whiskey down and took a sip of beer. Did you ever happen to know if a girl called Ruth ever used to come in here some time ago? he asked. Ruth? the bartender said. I don't even know *you*, champ. Drink up and take a walk, ok? You've had plenty.

■   ■   ■

It may well be that this fool wanted to say to this woman—let's call her Ruth, too—"Be careful! It's my heart."

Later that night, he thought that it would have been a good idea to remind Ruth's loudmouth belligerent yahoo husband that love has pitched his mansion in the place of excrement.

His wife wasn't home. Good news at last! He took a Tudor beer out of the refrigerator and got the bottle of Paul Jones down from the cupboard. The prince of beers, he said. The king of whiskeys. The new taste of modern luxury, old fellow! Then he sat down in the living room and lighted a cigarette. The bird of time has but a little way to flutter, Ruth, he said.

He could call Amelia. She used to wear a pearl choker with her black dress.

It has not been explained how this drunken fool got Ruth's number, since he did not know her married name. It has, however, been commented on by an astute copy editor that neither Ruth nor her loudmouth belligerent yahoo husband asked, "How did you get this number?"

DEAREST BELOVED,

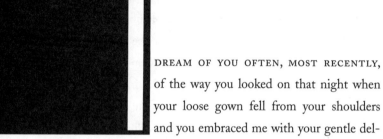

DREAM OF YOU OFTEN, MOST RECENTLY, of the way you looked on that night when your loose gown fell from your shoulders and you embraced me with your gentle delicate arms and kissed me, so sweetly. I can still hear your lovely whispering voice, "Dear heart, how do you like this?" *That* was no dream, no, I lay wide awake, but now I have little more than dreams. Everything that we had together is gone, changed, because of my gentleness perhaps, a gentleness which led, curiously, to your forsaking me. And yet I still love you, for love is love for beggars as for kings, as the saying has it, and love doesn't change because the circumstances that surround it change, no, it is like a fixed star. That is to say, my love is as it always was, even though your love has ceased to be, but, perhaps, perhaps, not ceased forever? You are my true love, you have my heart. Wake, love, to this fact, and please give yourself a moment to listen to the cheerful birds singing, singing, caroling of love! Don't be as unkind as man's ingratitude, or a proof that loving is mere folly.

Where, where *are* you? And where is your heart roaming? Please come home to me.

Every wise man, and every wise man's son, knows that love is for now, for the present, not for the hereafter. What is to come is unknown, and still unsure. When you were just twenty, and I used to say to you, "Come and kiss me, sweet," wherever we were, at parties, the movies, in the park or on the street, anywhere, you'd blush and laugh, but you will surely recall that you always *did* kiss me, when I reminded you, lightly, to be sure, that youth is a quality that will not endure. I know that you remember this. You were made all of light in those days, and the pure beams of that light scorched me, I'm afraid, not that I didn't welcome such sweet torture. I would welcome it still if you could tell me where all those past years are, where they went, those years so full of laughter and loving that are now as lost as a falling star. I still remember you as true and fair and honest, I still see the beauty of your face, like a heavenly paradise, and stupidly, often, all too often, I think that we might meet anywhere, just down the street, in the market, even next door! I thought that our love would never die, never decay, I thought that we were made, I confess it, that we were *invented* by such a love, I thought that our love somehow proved that we were—I don't quite know how to put this—mysterious. Do you know what I mean?

Oh dearest, please come back to me, or, at least, please reply to this letter. Give me a little hope, allow yourself, once again, to be desired, let me tell you, once again, how sweet and fair you are. I will love you until the world ends, until it is destroyed by flood or fire, until the whole world turns to coal! But we don't, now, have enough world, or enough time to see how, as you once said, "things will work out." At our backs, every minute, every second, time hurries on and in front of us is eternity, like a vast desert of loneliness. So let's devour this time, let's put our strength and our sweetness together, as we used to do. *Please* write or call. As it is, I admit, openly, that your absence has displaced my mind so that it is quite hopelessly locked into endless dreams of you.

As ever, my Beloved, good night, with a soft lullaby,
Your devoted, enamored, and faithful friend.

Dear friend:

Thanks for your recent letter. I enjoyed it, and think that the writing is wonderful, just as writing. But you don't quite engage that crucial faculty of response in me that must be engaged in order for me to respond as I feel I should respond to wonderful writing. You seem sure of yourself, but you're not getting it across to me, you don't manage to "jolt" me into taking a fresh view of our relationship. You, as always, have a good, though perhaps obsessive, sense of the past, and you often manage to convey marvelous emotional effect, but in the end your recollection of what we "had" together seems, I'm afraid, rather flat. I'm sorry.

In addition, your letter seems much too long, and I could not, for the life of me, unravel its real purpose, which is, perhaps, my failing. You seem, as always, obsessed with repetitions and, to be blunt, "fancy phrases," which are not really what I'm looking for right now, verbally speaking. Despite these objections, it's clear that what you do well you do *really* well, but my question, in the last analysis, is: Why did you write this? You've always had a talent for conversation, the "gift of gab," as an old, wise editor I once knew liked to say—she was a spark plug of a woman, indeed, in what was a man's world!—but I just did not *feel* this letter, chatty though it is. It seems full of repetitions, and for what you have to say, or plead, the letter's inordinate length really can't be justified. In a word, it is much too long.

I won't go into any unwanted song and dance concerning my view of our past relationship and your obsessions with the past and my physical person—I always told you these things, but you never listened to me. I can only say, as objectively as possible, that your letter, much like the last unfortunate months of our relationship, is neither engaging nor exhilarating. Indeed, I found myself struggling to read it all the way through, given its inordinately "poetic" language and its needless repetitions. In a way, it's an amazing letter, because you occasionally manage to make pain and paranoia funny as hell, but, finally, I just got bored. I'm sorry. Somehow, the gist, the real "heart" of your message cannot survive the irony of its presentation, I'm sorry to say. Perhaps it's the repetitiveness of the themes that damages your sincerity. I believe you, I do, really, when you say that you love me, but a letter that wishes to convey such a sentiment, such a passion, should do more than just say so. It should be a virtually perfect stunner. As it is, some of your phrases tickled my somewhat perverse and perhaps even "vulgar" sense of humor, an effect that I strongly doubt you intended. But then I may be wrong, since I could not figure out the purpose of your letter: Why, why did he do this? I kept asking myself, to the point of almost obsessive repetition. You are quite successful at conveying certain emotional states, if that was your intention, but you never allowed me to take a fresh "look" at our relationship, which is presented as rather flat and tame from its very inception, although I—and you—know better. You can, however, when you wish, convey strong emotional effects, repetitious though they may be.

I'm disappointed not to be coming back to you with an offer to touch base again with you. You know that I've always been a big "fan" of yours, even during those times when you were obsessed with lists of "fancy phrases." I know that I was supposed to like, or at least admire, those lists, but I was never really able to get into them. They were, of course, occasionally powerful and intriguing, but they were also somewhat paranoid and compulsive. I regret to say that I am not at all comfortable at the thought of reviving our friendship, relationship, what have you. I feel, strongly, that a decision to do so would be a disservice to both of us. Your letter, despite its length and, if I may be forgiven for saying so, its obsessive repetitiousness, has its poignant beauties, but it is also dark and claustrophobic and extremely narrow in scope. I might even go so far as to say that I found it full of a kind of disguised, benign unpleasantness. I don't think, really, my old friend, that you desire a resumption of what you call "strengthened sweetness," when such a relationship does not suit my particular needs at the present time.

As you will recall, I'm sure, I did all that I could for our relationship for nearly a decade, only to see it dwindle into a charade of unpleasantness on your part. Our separation, at the end of that experience, left much to be desired. I may be dead wrong, but the emotional effect of that separation was one that only a person with a perverse sense of the comic aspects of life would want to experience again. And that does not describe me, as you know. I did feel a twinge reading your letter, for although it is repetitiously obsessive and darkly paranoid, it is ashine, here and there, with your talent for expression and the *mot juste*. And although I am, more often than not, befuddled by your poetic phrases, they occasioned a number of emotionally wrenching memories. I have, as you know, great admiration for you still, and for your courage in writing. I regret to say, however, that I do not wish to see you again. I'm sorry. Please do not write again, unless you feel that you have something fresh and interesting to convey, a "new and different" offer, so to speak.

Sincerely,

Your friend

■　■　■

Although these stiff, even stilted and wooden letters are supposed to evoke a modern world that is at once badoom as well as bara-boom, it may be noted, in objection, that among the fancy phrases sorely missed are "I'll never smile again," "Shoot if you must this old gray head," and "I saw a groundhog lying dead, Dead lay he." Devoted Friend forgot to add, or, perhaps, insert them.

"Harry, how about another coffee over here, OK?"

What if it were to be revealed that these stiff, stilted, and wooden letters were exchanged between Donald and Dolores?

"Here's your coffee, friend," Harry says, carefully noting that the friend so addressed is not Donald, who has long since moved out of the neighborhood—as has Dolores.

"I am putting a pound to win on Small Advance in the fourth at Gulf Stream," Harry says. "Do you want to come in for another pound? At eight to five, it is a nice, comfortable price."

Would Dolores of the dark eyes and deep-golden skin and the face of Tibullus's Delia ever have written such a caitiff, whorish let-ter? Even to Donald?

NB: "These letters can only be thought of as the most elementary exercises in the epistolary. They are, even at best, stiff, stilted, and wooden. Their author, student though he or she may be, would do well to consider a career in handicapping, under the able tutelage of Harry the waiter."

Clarity, neatness, and thoroughness

E WAS RAISED A ROMAN CATHOLIC, AND while not relentlessly devout, was a good Catholic, heard mass every Sunday and on all Holy Days of Obligation, went to Confession and received the Eucharist a few times a year, regularly performed his Easter Duty, and had been an excellent catechism student as a boy, receiving a Commendation of Scholarship certificate from Monsignor Patrick J. O'Hara of Our Lady of Angels R.C. Church. He went on at least four retreats, ultimately joined the Knights of Columbus, and never, or at least rarely, took the name of the Lord in vain. At Brooklyn Technical High School, he excelled in his studies, and showed a special gift for organic chemistry. His laboratory notebooks were exemplary for their clarity, neatness, and thoroughness, and were, as a matter of fact, famous throughout the school. He was a Boy Scout, joining Troop 93 and becoming a member of the Eagle Patrol. He became, in time, a Junior Assistant Scoutmaster, then an Assistant Scoutmaster, and progressed rapidly from Tenderfoot to

Eagle Scout with two Silver Palms, earning, finally, thirty-seven merit badges, a record for the troop. He was a dishwasher and then an assistant counselor and then a counselor at Ten Mile River Scout Camp, where he won the TMR badge, qualifying for additional awards in aquatics, crafts, nature studies, and woodsmanship. In his third summer at Ten Mile River, he was selected for the Order of the Arrow, a secret honor society based upon Indian lore and practices. He attended at least eight camporees and jamborees, and at the age of sixteen became an Explorer Scout. He went to Brooklyn College for a year as a full-time day student, then switched to night college because of the necessity of earning a living in order to assist his mother and father, both of whom were drunks. It took him seven years to earn a B.S. in Chemistry. He was drafted into the Army and became a Military Policeman, stationed, in that capacity, at Fort Dix, Fort Lee, and Fort Leonard Wood. After being discharged from the Army in 1955, he fell in love with a beautiful neighborhood girl, Isabelle Piro, who was beginning to develop a very successful career as a high-fashion model. She was killed in an automobile crash on the Gowanus Expressway at 4:30 on a Sunday morning, and it was generally known that she had been blind drunk, driving at well over eighty, and completely naked under her dress, with her underwear, some of it semen-stained, in her handbag. He began to drink heavily after quarreling wildly with her parents over a nonexistent letter that he insisted she'd left for him. He joined the Lions, the American Legion, the Book of the Month Club, and the Confraternity of Christian Doctrine, all the while working as a laboratory assistant for IBM, a job that demanded virtually nothing from him. He then abruptly fell in love with the wife of one of his boyhood friends, and although she performed fellatio on him on an irregular basis, she would not go to bed with him, nor even consider leaving her husband. He asked her once to meet him, naked underneath her clothes but with her underwear in her handbag, and she told him that he was beginning to scare her and not to call anymore. He joined A.A., although, as a Catholic snob, he despised what he thought of as their humble, regular-guy God. He succeeded in his attempt at sobriety, but gave the organization no credit, since he never went to meetings after his fabricated tales of drunken degradation were accepted without question. As he began to dry out, he, oddly enough, was fired, and got another job, much like the first, in a lab in Long Island City. He became the Scoutmaster of a newly formed troop, and was soon adulterously involved with the absurdly thin wife of the pastor of the Norwegian Lutheran Church in whose basement the troop met every Friday evening. One night, after the boys had been dismissed and sent home, he was fucking Mrs. Ingebretsen, whom he sometimes called, with vague affection, "Bones," on the desk in the tiny closet of a room that had been designated the "troop library," because of the single shelf of unread books behind the desk, when one of the new members of the troop, a gawky boy who had not yet procured a uniform, opened the door, his *Handbook for Boys* in his hand, and a question, never asked, poised behind his open mouth. That was that, and he left the troop, began to drink again, and flirted with Zen, just before joining the War Resisters League and a pornographic video club, I.C. Pussie Video Sales. For a time, he became an obsessive masturbator, but then grew bored with orgasms. At a rally in Union Square against hate and violence, etc., he fell in love with Joan Baez, or someone who looked and sounded like her, who was singing of peace and fellowship and against most, but not all, rich people. He left the square, humming some old Pete Seeger warhorse, and composing, in his mind, the perfect letter to Miss Baez, when, just as he was completing his witty postscript, he was hit by a Checker cab at Tenth Street and Broadway, directly in front of Grace Church, and died on his way to St. Vincent's.

■　■　■

Obviously missing from this "sketch" (not my word, I assure you!) is anything that this man may have said, at any time, to anybody. It would have been interesting to know, for instance, the content of his remarks, if any, to Mrs. Ingebretsen and Donald Fritjofsen (the gawky boy), on the occasion of their common embarrassment, and, too, his comments on the matter to Pastor Ingebretsen.

It is to be hoped that this man practiced safe sex in "the age of AIDS," shared responsibility for birth control whenever he "got lucky," eschewed cigarettes and all other tobacco products, knowing, as he did, that they are far, far deadlier than massive carpet-bombings and low-level napalm strikes, avoided red meat, salt, refined sugar, and saturated fats, and got plenty of exercise, despite the weeping that regularly convulsed him.

Modern Business English; The Life of the Spider; Mark, the Match Boy; Fables in Slang; Dave Dawson with the Air Corps; Penrod Jashber; Selections from the Homilies of Pastor Pietsch; The Boy Ranchers in the Desert; A Mother's Prayer; Tom Sawyer; Best Loved Poems of the American People; The Curse of Darwin; The Ordeal of Harriet Marwood, Governess; Letters for All Occasions; A Heap o' Livin'; A Pocket History of England; The Adventures of Ulysses.

Joan Baez, or the singer who looked like her, could not hold a candle to Isabelle Piro insofar as feminine beauty is concerned; an indication, perhaps, of this unfortunate man's mental decline.

"Checker cabs are gone, you know? And if we play our cards right we can get rid of the age of AIDS, too, you know? If we talk to the Checker cab guys who got them out, I mean, who got rid of them, the cabs, you know what I mean?"

"Talks like a guy with a paper asshole," Tommy Azzerini remarks.

E HAD BEEN, FOR MANY YEARS, INTRUSIVE, selfish, callous, controlling, petty, and child-ish, and given to prevarication, forgetfulness, and maddening self-justification. An almost intolerable clod of a husband, whose smug egotism made him a good target for his wife's occasional, unexpected, and thoroughly justified countermeasures. One night, when his wife asked him to slice a tomato for their supper, he took a large, ripe tomato out of the refrigerator, and noticed that there was a half-tomato there as well, covered tightly in shrink wrap. He took that out, too. He had sliced this half-tomato and was beginning to slice the whole tomato, when his wife asked him why, why he'd sliced the half-tomato when she had expressly asked him to slice *a* tomato, a *whole* tomato. With the counterfeit, smug patience that often causes brutal assaults and even murders to be committed upon those who pretend its possession, he explained that he'd sliced the half-tomato and would now slice *half* of the whole tomato, so that they could "use up," was his phrase, the older, so to speak,

half-tomato, and save half of the newer, so to speak, whole tomato. He indeed employed the phrase, "so to speak," in itself a maddened attacker's defensible justification for battery. He quietly noted that if it was her *heart's desire*, he would slice the entire whole tomato, should she feel that a tomato and a half would not be too much for supper, considering, no, knowing of the *wonderful meal* that she was certainly preparing. She asked him why he thought, why in Christ's name did he think, what gave him the goddamned idea that she wanted him to slice the goddamned half-tomato to begin with. Huh? He said, almost bloated with reasonableness, that it seemed a perfectly reasonable "operation to perform," yes, he said that, that is: to "use up" the half a tomato that had been in the refrigerator since the day before yesterday, losing flavor and juiciness and vitamins and fucking minerals, whatever the hell they have, to eat the thing, made perfect sense to him. Did he ever, ever, ever, she asked, stop to think that maybe she was saving that half a tomato for something, that she had plans for it? Plans?, he said. Plans? *Plans?* He said that if she indeed had, ah, plans, big plans for the fucking half a fucking tomato, could she not use the half-tomato that would be left after he finished slicing the whole tomato? Couldn't she? She told him that it wasn't his business to decide for her which half a tomato she wanted to use. To use, he said, to implement your *big plans.* She said that her decisions were her decisions and that if she wanted to take all the miserable goddamned tomatoes and throw them out the window, it was her business! He said that he hadn't intended to make decisions for her, God forbid, he simply thought that blah blah and sensible blah, that he thought that it was something that she herself would do, blah. You have no idea, you have no idea, you don't have any idea what I'd do about it, you have no idea what I'd do about anything, that's the trouble, that's always been the trouble, and wasn't, she added, wasn't it about time that he seriously started looking for a job?, with his Master's in sociology? And did it ever occur to him while he watched the ball game that she didn't feel like eating a stale tomato, a dried-out tomato, that she wanted a fresh tomato? Or was the ball game too intellectually demanding? She said that when she asked him to do something she wished that he would, just once, do it, and not do something else and then spend three hours trying to convince her that that's what he thought she wanted him to do. I ask you to cut a tomato, *cut a tomato!* At which, with a small, hapless smile, he asked her, whining, whether she wanted him to continue slicing the whole tomato, or just half of it, and what about the sliced half-tomato now? He stood, slightly slumped, as if crushed in spirit, unmanned, impotent, a posture which his arrogant sneer belied. She said that he could do what he wanted to do, the king of the kitchen, the reader of minds, the weaver of dreams, he could slice, not slice, stick the tomatoes up his ass slice by slice, send them to the goddamned stupid millionaire bastard Pittsburgh Cubs. As for her, she didn't want any tomatoes or any supper, for that matter! She washed and dried her hands and walked out of the kitchen. What about the chicken? he asked. What about the chicken? I said, what about the chicken? And the rice? The sliced tomato on the cutting board had the placid look of all blameless objects that have been swiftly carried across time so as to bewilder and confound.

■　■　■

This is a variation on a certain kind of common marital quarrel. The elements are simple and faintly absurd, yet they must be understood as counters that have negligible literal value. The quarrel, that is, is metonymic, as are all inane quarrels. Such quarrels are very much like dreams. You remember dreams.

Elements that might enrich this quarrel are many and diverse, the most interesting being any that have to do with the past, where all resentments and failures and regrets lie in a state of horrible suspended animation, ready, at the slightest nudge, to wake and shamble out of the darkness, unchanged, unchanging, terrible to behold.

"The tomato episode" featured RUTH and HER LOUDMOUTH BELLIGERENT YAHOO HUSBAND. We don't let anybody get away with anything.

"Now's the time to fall in love," Eddie Cantor says. As it was in 1931, so it is now and ever shall be, love without end. Amen.

"It says on this note that I've been asked to read," adds Eddie Cantor, "'This could, too, be Dolores and her husband, the plumber.'"

E HEARS OF A MAN, AS ONE WILL, OR HE "dreams up" a man, and, elaborating upon a simple notion, places him within a storm of sexual pleasure with his first wife of some three months, pleasure so intense that the newlyweds break the bed on which they have been making the fabled beast. Much loving laughter ensues, life cynically proffers itself in its lying guise as a bowl of cherries, and then goes blundering on.

Some years later, the man, in an adulterous episode in a hotel, or a motel, thinks of that evening of the broken bed and recalls that it was a Sunday, as is this particular evening of, as they say, illicit love. He commemorates the fact by embracing the cliché of the post-coital cigarette. "I can't believe that I'm actually thinking of this cigarette as a cliché," he says to the girl. "That's being self-conscious to a fare-thee-well, right, kid? It's life imitating kitsch imitating the movies imitating life." She smiles at him, and he realizes that she has no idea what "kitsch" means. God knows, she's nice enough, but she worries, she has told him, about what will happen to the Beatles if George should leave. Well, if she doesn't know what kitsch is, she can't know who Fats Navarro is, either. "Fats Navarro?" he says to her. She smiles at him and asks for a drag. Oh shit, it *is* a scene from a lame slice-of-life movie, chock full of intense looks, precocious children, and New York stoops. [It was a Sunday evening, absolutely, when he and his first wife broke the bed.] Don't forget the badinage in the laundromat!

The years pass, he and his first wife divorce, the usual grief with the two children, the fucking puppet shows and zoo and trips to Coney Island, the strained jokes with the new boyfriend, an optometrist of enormous sensitivity, the prick. He remarries, and after a brief time, begins to commit adultery again. The girls with whom he grapples and sweats and fails and lies don't know who Fats Navarro is, either. They don't know who Red Garland is, or Lester Young, or Ziggy Elman or Kid Ory. They never heard of the Roxy or the Strand or "Brooklyn Boogie" or the old Battery Park Aquarium or Pete Reiser or the Third Avenue El or Grant's or Toffenetti's. Some of them have been to the Bronx, but not too many. They don't know about Vito Marcantonio or William O'Dwyer or Joe Adonis. They don't know anything. "Bye, Bye, Blackbird," he says to one of them one night as he puts her in a cab. She smiles at him, that Ohio smile, that editorial assistant smile, that Godforsaken Shakespeare-in-the-Park smile that they all have to hand. Now, when he's in bed with one of these girls, he often has to put up with the fatal-secondhand-smoke cliché that tends to ride in on the back of the post-coital ciga-rette cliché. These young women, who have no idea of Art Tatum's actuality, or that Dexter Gordon at his best can make your heart stop, think that a whiff or two of this evil smoke will cut years off their fulfilling, really peppy lives. They are content to flirt with chlamydia, gonorrhea, syphilis, herpes, and AIDS, but fear the fragrant weed as if it is the Foul Fiend himself, in miniature static disguise. One, a stunning girl who sustained herself on yogurt and dried fruit, called his Marlboro a "death stick." This is true. But more troubling than the dippy health concerns of these glowing, utterly amoral lawyers and consultants and junior brokers, these persons with promising careers in creative "fields" like magazine publishing and advertising, is the fact that each bed that he finds himself in—not a salubrious phrase, to be sure—reminds him of the broken bed, now, of course, rotting, figuratively, in the far-off past. He thinks to call his first wife about this, stupid as such a thought may be, but she has long been remarried, to, as he recalls, Mark, the civil engineer, has moved to some grim, sunny outpost crammed with Friendly People, and loathes him. He cannot speak of this to his current wife, for obvious reasons. So he keeps this malaise to himself, in the same box with Lundy's and Steeplechase.

The man who heard or invented this story, such as it is, later hears that the pitiful adventurer has died, and that he believed that his deathbed had broken. This pleased him. The deceased was identified as a fellow named either Teddy or Perry, and there should be someone who can confirm this, someone to whom a letter of inquiry might be sent, at some address like "Chez Freddy" or "The Blue Front" or, simply, "the island." Perhaps the inquiry might be directed to Orville or Jackie Lang, but they, too, must be dead by now. Others who might know are anonymously strewn across the playful, desolate land.

■　■　■

The broken bed was located in the bedroom of a four-room apartment in a small brick building on Woodside Avenue in Brooklyn. The motel was the Castle Rest Inn, some two miles from the Jersey entrance to the Lincoln Tunnel. The "Bye, Bye, Blackbird" girl was put in the cab on the corner of Bleecker and Charles Streets. Chez Freddy burned down and on the site is a Christian bookstore, Gethsemane Books and Videos. The Blue Front is now Lakeview Video, after a Radio Shack in that location failed. Nobody seems to have any idea to what island "the island" might refer.

Loue makes men sayle from shore to shore,
So doth Tobaccoe,
Tobaccoe, Tobaccoe,
Sing sweetely for Tobaccoe,
Tobaccoe is like loue.

"It's a shame that a person who is wholly uninterested in Beatles lore should suggest, by literary example, that smoking is acceptable. And where is Woodside Avenue, for God's sake?"

["Life Is Just a Bowl of Cherries," words by Lew Brown, music by Ray Henderson, was published in 1931, when the Depression was still being characterized by Herbert Hoover as a passing aberration. This was the same Mr. Hoover who, at about that time, noted that many people had left good jobs to sell apples on the street, so profitable was the latter undertaking. What a sweetheart.]

"The banal motif (e.g., the post-coital cigarette) is not precisely defined by the word 'kitsch'. . . ."

—Ancilla to Theory Studies, 1984.

AD HIS MOTHER NOT GIVEN HIM CREAM
of tomato soup for lunch every day for four
years, three months, one week, and two days,
it is possible that he would not have married
the neighborhood whore. Had his mother not got a restraining
order against his father, which prohibited the latter from coming
within fifty yards of him, it is probable that he would not have
become a dedicated drunk. Had he not got "pink eye" at the
Tompkinsville swimming pool, it is likely that he would not have
become a truck driver. Had she not torn open her forearm on a
rusty hurricane fence, it is not too much to assume that she would
not have, some years later, contracted poliomyelitis. Had she not
unaccountably lost her panties during a festive day at George C.
Tilyou's Steeplechase, it can be conjectured that she would have
graduated from a "good college." Had he not drunk a third of the
contents of his father's quart of Kinsey Silver Label Blended
Whiskey, he, perhaps, might have become a priest. Had he not, in
1950, bought a 1937 Chevrolet for sixty dollars, he, maybe, would

have bought, in 1982, a 1982 Mercedes Benz. Had he not had eleven tubercular ribs removed, it's a cinch that he would never have written a novel. Had he not been seduced by an ugly young man in Owl's Head Park, it is a surety that he would not have been seduced by a handsome young man at a Grove Street party. Had he not masturbated relentlessly, obsessively, and "at the drop of a hat," he would surely not have burst into flames while sound asleep. Had he not regularly tormented and thrashed younger children in the schoolyard of P.S. 102, he would have absolutely avoided his fate as a palooka club fighter. Had he not had his eye injured in a fall down a stairway of Fort Hamilton High School, he, without a doubt, would have had a long career as a noncommissioned officer in the 2nd Armored Division. Had she not been sexually exploited and slandered by a petty criminal, she would, doubtlessly, have resisted the lure of heroin. Had he not blasphemously prayed to God and His Blessed Mother to supply him with "bevies" of lascivious girls with whom he could have his debauched way, he, conceivably, might have avoided "problems" with various sexually transmitted diseases. If she had not hated her mother and father throughout all the years of her childhood, adolescence, puberty, and young womanhood, she would have, presumably, resisted the call of the convent. Had he not been fascinated by ships and the sea, it is evident that he would not have been killed in action aboard the U.S.S. *Portland.* Had she not lied, regularly and flagrantly, in the confessional, she would certainly have embraced atheism. Had he not seriously injured his hip while roughhousing in the Loew's Alpine, he would, clearly, have become a professional baseball player of minor-league proficiency. Had she not masturbated with various kitchen implements, most notably a wooden potato masher, she would have definitely resigned herself to her husband's indifferent carnal performances. Had he not eaten, laughingly, a Baby Ruth just fifteen minutes before receiving the Eucharist at the altar rail of Our Lady of Perpetual Help R.C. Church, he would, indeed, have escaped the lightning bolt that killed him on the way home. Had he been aborted, as his mother wished, he would not, positively, have had the opportunity to shoot to death two Armenian shopkeepers and a policeman of Irish extraction one hot July afternoon. Had he not smashed a plate-glass window of Shiffman's Toys, he would have become a successful corporate attorney and rapist. Had he not been dangerously frivolous in his play with a Gilbert chemistry set given him for Christmas, there is a good chance that he would have been famously unsuccessful in a "search for the cure" for AIDS. Had his mother not suffered his rage, insults, and contumely, it is not beyond expectation to assume that he would never have developed into a sadistic killer. Had he not become frightened when he tried on his mother's underwear, he would, presumably, have become a contented, if boring homosexual, or, as he would have learned to say, "queer."

■　　■　　■

Each of these linkages can be added to or changed. The mysteries of causes and effects are beyond understanding.

"Or not worth understanding, buddy."

"Whore," in the present context, may be read as "tramp" or "slut." No professionalism is suggested by the use of the word. It may even be read as "mam'selle" by Frankie Laine fans, among whom, believe it or not, are a number of boring homosexuals, or "queers."

This diversion, here indited for your pleasure, may ultimately be the cause of your divorce. Don't ask me. It's quite probable that had

I not written this "chapter," I would have written a different one. So much for the inevitability of art.

"What do you mean?"

Or the inevitability of anything else, for that matter. Save death.

"What do you mean? Death? Who's Frankie Laine?"

Certain troops, discharged into civilian life from the bosom of the 2nd Armored Division, find that they are Nervous From The Service.

Georgene liked Frankie Laine and knew all the words to his "Mam'selle," "Black and Blue," "Mule Train," and, perhaps unforgivably, "Ghost Riders in the Sky." That was before she went to Barnard and met Gilbert C. Grove, a man who worshiped F.R. Leavis and E.M. Forster. Nothing to be done with Gilbert!

It may be of passing interest to note that the phrase, "queer studies," if enunciated as an anapest, takes on a different meaning from the meaning projected when the phrase is enunciated as a dactyl.

HE CRIED AND SULKED WHEN EVERYBODY was dressed and ready to leave for the park, and later in the day tried to push her half-brother in front of a bus, just a joke, well, she was laughing. She said that her mother's lover and the lover before him and the lovers before him whom she could not quite recall had groped and fondled and stroked and fingered and raped her more times than she could count, aided and abetted by the silence of her mother. Her brother was a dope fiend, a speed freak, an alcoholic, a man who couldn't keep a woman, even those skinny, dirty, hopeless schmecker drunk unemployables he got mixed up with. I'll write soon, she always said, and send pictures of the family! And pictures of this and of that, the swell husband, the really great little house that she just loved in sunny and relaxed and laid-back and really beautiful Northern California, baking in the paralyzing heat of the Sacramento Valley, a heat that was the tangible counterpoint to the weirdness and barely concealed despair of that huge, hysterical state, crammed with maniacs wildly and grinningly unhappy, and hypnotized by regular explosions of blood in the ruthless sunshine, under the unsettling blue skies, when, of course, it wasn't pouring rain for months on end. This really *great* weather! made her write even less frequently. She divorced her husband, the impossible dumbbell, after he had, on a number of occasions, suggested that maybe she could get a job? But how could she get a job, when the incredibly difficult pregnancy and ensuing stillbirth that had almost killed her, that had her on the very edge of death!, yes, she had been right on the edge of a death like nobody else's death, a death as grim and terrible as, well, you know. Fifteen years earlier it had been a muggy, gray kind of day, when she cried and sulked and demanded to be begged and pleaded with and implored to please, please, oh *please* can we, let's, please, can we go out to the park? Everybody is dressed and ready to go and it's almost three o'clock, please? And after this intense look, like, into the very face of death, how could she get a job, considering her ensuing, insistent, recurring, and incurable ectopic pregnancies, her six dilation and curettage procedures by bloodthirsty butcher doctors who couldn't even speak English, or was it seven?, her vaginal hemorrhages, bleeding hemorrhoids, back pains, endless infections of liver and kidneys and bladder and spine and what do you call it?, coccyx, and then the terrible discovery that her spinal infection was chronic and progressive. The dim son of a bitch machinist in the National Guard who got her pregnant after her husband had angrily departed, but not, oh no, not before he killed the dog and cat, uprooted the garden, tore the gorgeous black Naugahyde couch to shreds, and stole the best lamp with the mauve silk shade, the wedding present from her dearest mom, and did other things that she'd think of soon! This machinist, a guy who seemed like a really sweet man who had a nice little power boat, but also a bitch of a nagging shrew of a battleax of a wife, but he wouldn't leave her, despite what he called "the fruit of their love" that lay in her womb an innocent, and despite her threats to *tell* the fucking cunt of a wife!, and then one day they had just god-damn moved away, and then the near-fatal recurring hemorrhages began, and the trauma of her history of sexual, physical, moral, mental, emotional, religious, and, uh, ethical abuses almost killed her, yes. And then there was the trauma of trying to live with the horrible memories of her ex-boss, the guinea bastard, her ex-boss, who had given her all the insulting, menial tasks in the air-conditioning store and repair shop, where she had gritted her teeth and got a job despite the rivers of blood that regularly gushed out of her generative organs and the spinal pain so bad that she wanted to scream right there at her tiny desk in real, actual agony. The traumatic recollection, too, was uppermost in her mind of him giving her that look that the Modern Living and Arts section of the newspaper called the "male gauge" or something like that, and the nightmarish horror of her shame at him saying that she looked very pretty in her new short skirt and him touching her on the forearm with a leer and another, even dirtier male gauge. She had to quit, and was thinking of suing, but a guy she met at a bar told her that her post-stress syndrome would be hard to prove after she told the guy that she'd gone out to dinner with the boss and did a few other things, too, maybe about oh, maybe twenty times. And anyway, how could she possibly sue and get involved with lawyers with her new pregnancy, when she could only get relief from her infected arthritic spinal column and kidneys by lying flat on the kitchen floor for hours, anything, anything to ease the agony of her corroding bones and ligaments and things. On top of that, she began to hemorrhage again a little bit and then came the blinding migraines and the brain-tumor fears. God knows why she didn't lose the child, the poor little bastard love-child, nor why she didn't die, the obstetrician said that in thirty-five years of experience hers was the most difficult birth that he'd ever seen. That rotten bum of a beer-swilling son of a bitch of a fake soldier and his bitch of a whore of a wife had nothing to do with her pulling through! Her mother's house was the only place left to go now, since to go to work at some rotten minimum-wage job with her ovaries irritated and swollen and the new baby and his demands was out of the question, it was a place to take stock, right, even though her mother had looked the other way all during those years when she'd been as good as raped, and those, well, those, ah, episodes were most likely the cause of her infected kidneys, she'd read about things like that happening in the paper. The baby was so cute and pretty and a love, but let's face it, a real pain in the *ass*, she couldn't stand, that is, her nerves couldn't stand the kid's howling and the colic and the feedings and the dirty, stinking diapers, Jesus Christ, come on!, she just had to get out three or four times a week, anyway, for a few hours, and see some of her old friends and that big guy who used to be a Marine and who worked for the phone company. She wrote to a California girlfriend that the baby was adorable and as smart as a whip, and that her mother was helping her out a little bit once in a while, and soon she'd start interviewing for a job in her field, office management, that was her specialty, of course, or perhaps management and senior accounting, although she *was* a little rusty, her fathead of an ex-husband forbidding her to go to work no matter how many times she'd shown him the household budget figures and how much better off they'd be if only, oh well!, that's water under the bridge, and, too, she had taken a long time to get over her sexual traumas of her childhood abuse and the guinea ex-boss's rubbing up against her in the office and the sudden terrible hemorrhagic spinal infections with pus leakage, and the kid shitting and pissing and crying all day and all night, and then her dope-addict brother coming around to steal a few dollars from their mom while she was out, pretending to care about the baby, and nodding at the kitchen table the whole time. And it also looks as if I may be having my eleventh D and C, believe it or not, since I am in terrible abominal agony which is only relieved when I have a brief hemorrhage. OK. Pictures of the family on the way!

■ ■ ■

In the interests of fairness, it should be made clear that the depraved, departed husband of this suffering woman, according to records obtained, with considerable difficulty, some few years ago from HQ, III U.S. Army Corps, Fort Hood, Texas, was, upon his discharge from active duty, classified as NS-1, or, Nervous From The Service. This "nervous" state may well have contributed to his lack of understanding of his wife's emotional needs and her feelings of inadequacy and low self-esteem. This is a common occurrence, according to Captain Laurence O'Banion, AMEDS, not fully understood even by the Army.

"One wonders how the author of this exercise in barely disguised misogyny would like it if he received an unwanted compliment on *his* short skirt."

[The above paragraph is especially reprehensible, for it attempts to soften the misogyny of the chapter by the utilization of what is, essentially, an adolescent joke, and one that is, not so incidentally, wholly insensitive to the emotional needs and occasional feelings of inadequacy of cross-dressing males. It also, by calling attention to its message by the use of quotation marks, pretends that the putative writer of the message is different from the actual writer of the message, that is, Gilbert Sorrentino; and that the sentiments and beliefs expressed by Gilbert Sorrentino are not his own, but those of the putative writer. To compound these absurdities, we have the very paragraph that you are reading, a paragraph which labors to remove Gilbert Sorrentino from that which Gilbert Sorrentino has already expressed; to remove Gilbert Sorrentino from that which the putative writer has already expressed; and to remove Gilbert Sorrentino from the authorship of this very paragraph. The fact that this paragraph has made mention of its purpose makes any recognition or condemnation of an exteriorized misogyny (for which, it appears, *nobody* may be held responsible) in the chapter or its addenda, disingenuous at best and dishonest at worst.]

MORAL: *Never Trust A Writer.*

"I wear women's clothes because, well, gee, they make me feel whole and complete and, well, fulfilled, and besides, they're much more comfortable than trousers and belts and big heavy shoes, ties, and so on. And, heck, if slipping into these things gives me a really terrific, you know, erection, that's just my body's way of compensating for my occasional feelings of inadequacy and low self-esteem and my mind's way of expressing, through my body, my deepest emotional needs as a gender-problematic being, you know?"

[The above paragraph is also reprehensible.]

 AS I UNDERSTAND IT, THIS WAS AT ABOUT the time that you got a part-time job as a bookkeeper at Anthanna Air Conditioning and Motorcycle?

A. Correct.

Q. You worked for a man you occasionally referred to as a "guinea bastard"?

A. Yes, well, but he, Tony Mari—

Q. No names need be mentioned, Miss.

A. Yes, I did, I'm sorry to say, and sometimes I called him a cruel person, too, and an insensitive person, irregardless of race, because he was often terrible and cruel to me on days when I was hemorrhaging massively with various infections and a distorted coccyx.

Q. What is, please, a "distorted coccyx"?

A. Distorted. Distorted, you know? Sort of like twisted, so that a typical sufferer has to lay down on the floor in agony.

Q. I'm still not clear on what—

My client is not a medical doctor! Let's just leave it at distorted, all right?

Q. Is your doctor's report, or letter, among these papers that you've submitted in support of your filing?

A. Right. Correct, yes. But he's a New York doctor and we, he, hasn't gotten the good files from the clinic and hospital in California, from my California doctors, who are recognized experts on infections and my type of distortions and hemorrhages. They have the good files, the case . . . things.

Q. You don't, then, are you saying that you don't then vouch for the accuracy or completeness of the medical information submitted here today through your attorney?

Don't answer that!

A. All I can assert is that my coccyx is just as the medical information says it is, just as distorted now as it has been since my ordeal at Anthanna, and that I have infectious bleeding and some swollen internal organs.

Q. Swollen internal organs? I don't seem to recall that you mentioned swollen internal organs earlier, or that, they, for that matter, are mentioned—

Can we expedite this deposition, please? My client had a hemorrhage just this morning on the way over here which I barely stanched all over the upholstery of my new BMW.

Q. I'm merely trying to determine what "swollen internal organs" your client is referring to, and just what "infectious bleeding" might be. Not to mention our old friend, "distorted coccyx."

Don't answer the question, and there's no need for you to be a wise guy, either. "Our old friend!"

Q. I didn't ask a question, sir. I am not asking at this time, a question, sir. I merely want—

Well, you're supposed to be asking questions, not "merely" making snideish comments.

Q. All right. We can clear up these details of, ah, description later. Fine. Now, Miss, you claim that your employer often leered at you?

A. It is a demeaning memory of absolute horrible fear and humiliation that totally ruined my ability to do my tasks, as well as making a very bad climate in the work area and also place.

Q. Of what did this leer consist? I'm sorry, let me be clearer. Can you, that is, describe this leer?

A. It is very difficult to remember clearly because of my current condition of post-dramatic stress, but it was a very dirty kind of look, as if he was looking improperly at my bosoms and private limbs and other organs right through my garments.

Q. Did he leer at you on what you might consider a regular basis, or were his leers irregular and occasional?

A. He began his objectionable leering activities from the minute I walked in the office every morning like he was looking, like Superman's x-ray vision, through my dress and intimate garments. He gazed a lot at me, all day, in fact, that's all I know, and I was rended terribly nervous.

Q. Had you ever apprised him of your discomfort and feelings of embarrassment and anger as the recipient of these suggestive leers?

A. He was my boss, the absolute boss, even though he was nothing but a greaseball pervert! Excuse me for that ethical slur, I'm sorry. I was, sir, deeply afraid that I'd lose my position and so tried to ignore his perverted activities even though the workplace atmosphere became intolerable for me. How I longed, really longed to talk to another woman about my boss, but the only other woman in the office was his sister-in-law, and she was a real bimbo, believe you me.

Q. All right, Miss. If you didn't talk with this sister-in-law there is no need to mention your opinion as to what you believed to be her loose morals. Your characterization of this woman as a "bimbo" somehow doesn't really . . . surprise me.

I object to the tone here taken, and the implication that these sexual tortures in the workplace can be brushed off, when, as scientific tests have shown, such experiences can cause victims to become completely disgusted with normal sex.

Q. Noted. All right. You have said that after your employer leered at you, he also subjected you to what you call the "male gaze." As a matter of fact, I think, yes, you just stated a few moments ago that your employer "gazed a lot" at you.

A. That is correct.

Q. Uh-huh. What is this male gaze? Can you describe it? Is it different from a leer? Is it more like a stare? An ogle? A glance? Is it, perhaps, a wink?

A. It's like here and now, yes!, here and now!, with YOU trying your leveled best to look up my skirt all morning, even though I am in considerable pain with my coccyx swollen and inflamed, and on the verge of a kind of emotional collapse, I am still a sexual object to the male gaze and dirty leer!

Q. I have not!—I have, Miss, I assure you, I have not been—this is outrageous!—trying to, good Lord!, trying to look up your skirt, I assure you!

A. Oh, really? You can hardly take your eyes off my limbs, as if it is not my right, a woman's right, to wear a short skirt and expect a gentleman to refrain from gazing so as to inflame his brutal lust! It is not my fault if my short skirt has given you an erection!

A. What!? What!? I am simply astonished at—again, I assure you, Miss, I have no intention of subjecting you to embarrassment, I'm outraged at your suggestion that—that—I'm outraged and insulted!

A. Well, perhaps I'm mistaken. Perhaps it's your glasses that make your eyes look all googly like they're popping out of your head staring.

Q. I'll . . . I'll accept that, Miss, as an apology.

That was not an apology! Let's not subject my client to any more patronizing cracks, all right?

Q. In your original complaint, you stated that your employer touched your leg above the knee? Would that be, would you say, would that be your thigh that he touched?

A. Yes, it was. He fondled my thigh both on the outside and the inner portion, while suggesting that we could go to the Acey-Five Motel and relax for a few hours, is what he called it, and then he suggested that I take a look at his aroused bulge in his pants, "take a gander at this prize," was his actual lewd remark.

Q. And yet, in your earliest complaint of this occurrence you stated that your employer, and I quote, "touched my forearm, like, my wrist, in a more than just friendly way." Is that correct?

A. Yes. But I also said that he fondled my thigh as he touched my wrist, and as he fondled and touched, he was also giving me the x-ray male gaze at my bosoms, so that I was filled with disgust and a terrible sense of not being valued for my bookkeeping contributions to the workplace, and that my career goals were not being respected. My morale plunged way down at that moment, especially since he left no doubt in my mind as to his intentions when he commented on the Acey-Five Motel, which everyone knows is a place for, well, let's say dates, and then shocked me by displaying his aroused state within his pants.

Q. Did your employer ever ask you to wear short skirts?

A. He very strongly suggested this to me, and once, while doing so, he handed me a pen in a filthy sexual manner, while he leered at my body and filled me with a traumatic fear that he would suddenly tell me a dirty joke or off-color anecdote. This pen episode was one that planted the nightmare seeds of post-dramatic stress that I suffer from today, along with an aggravation that is not good for my infected ectopic effects as well . . .

Plus there is the sudden hemorrhaging like in the car that I have mentioned and the chronic infection flare-ups.

Q. I'm well aware of your client's various ills, sir. I'm sorry, Miss, did you want to add something?

A. He also made suggestive and sexually explicit remarks about pulling up my skirt so that he could gaze at my distorted coccyx and see it for himself, and he made it clear that he wanted to do this in a cruel and immoral fashion.

Q. Didn't you, at the time of this occurrence, state that you hadn't played "doctor" in a long time, but it might be fun? And subsequent to this occurrence, while you continued to work and to get pay raises at Anthanna, you wore nothing but a diaper, bra, and high heels as The New Year at a year-end office party, did you not? And you also dated your employer, and even stayed overnight at his home on several occasions when his wife was out of town, isn't that true? And didn't you tell a fellow employee, the purchasing agent, that your employer was, and I quote, "a bad lay who could use some help in the hard-on department"? Aren't all these things true? And aren't there many other stories like these, most notably, perhaps, the "salami party" story?

I object, I object, I object to this bald-faced slander of my client, who has been martyred enough! This is a case of harassment, insult, and vile innuendoes concocted by this misogynist's cronies!

A. These things are all distorted a lot, and are not what they seem to be at all. And I would never use such gross language as what you just said, to the purchasing agent, speaking of which, she is a sex-crazy busybody divorcée, and who also runs to the boss with all the gossip, as she has a crush on him to beat the band. Talk about short skirts! Now, *she* looks like a real tramp!

Q. But you did date your employer, did you not?

A. I may have gone to dinner with him once or twice, but I was in a post-dramatic stress syndrome at the time from the shock of fondling and unwanted compliments concerning my physical nature and modes of dress, and I did not know in a responsible fashion what I was actually doing. My employer took advantage of me at these times, since I also had a brief amnesia-type condition that was caused by an internal spinal hemorrhage that came about through work-place stress. I actually thought that my employer was my pastor, Pastor Ingebretsen.

Q. The stenographer will see to it that that name does not get into the record? Thank you. Now, Miss. Did you ever stay at your employer's house while his wife was away, and while you, as a matter of fact, were still married?

A. I had, I have been told, arthritic brain swellings at the time.

Q. Is this a photograph of you and your employer in bed together at the Acey-Five Motel? And isn't this other woman, who is standing at the side of the bed, the purchasing agent of the company?

A. I think that I have to lay down now because of the agony of my spinal infection flaring up with stress factors, but I must first state without fear that my employer is a liar who leered at me with a gaze and violated my thighs and shocked me with crude jokes and remarks upon my clothing choices. He is also not above doctoring innocent photos. Now that's all for now, please.

Here, here! Let her lay down on the table! And you can keep your eyes and your hands to yourself, counselor!

Q. I *beg* your pardon?

■   ■   ■

"Writers who have little or no respect for their characters, or who actively dislike or disdain them to such a degree that even the most sympathetic reader finds herself unable to care for them, would be well advised to study and make critical notes on every story appearing in *The Atlantic Monthly* since 1970."

—*Crafting the Short Story,* 5th Edition.

How about *The New Yorker?*

"Too . . . hip?"

One wonders how the author of this exercise in barely disguised misogyny would like it if the nightmare seeds of post-dramatic stress were planted in *his* mind.

Speaking of "the author" of the above, it should be remarked that upon a first reading of the text, it seems glaringly apparent that the said text is imaginative, i.e., fictional. However, recent events make it clear that this is an accurate transcription of an actual deposition, the deposed being one Charlotte Ryan. Further investigation has revealed that Anthanna Air Conditioning and Motorcycle is part of a business consortium that also includes Aquatic Ship Scaling, Inc.

THE SCENE IS SO BANAL AS TO MAKE ONE weep in desperation, and yet, what an overwhelming sense of life!

"Nice of you to give your weekend, Ms. Paluka."

"Oh, that's all right, Mr. Pepp, I'm very interested in this account, it's a real learning experience working on it. I'm grateful, really, for the opportunity."

Surely, Mr. Pepp meant "give up."

How careful she'd been about the clothes she'd packed for this working weekend—including her nightclothes! Sensual, she thought, yes, but not frilly. Expensive.

(Earlier, assuming that these two savvy and aggressive reps of a savvy and aggressive microchip firm did not just *appear* on the page without rambling through a lot of actual life, a bartender in the hotel lounge might well have been permitted a regular-guy cliché.)

In the hotel room, Mr. Pepp's, since he is the senior junior assistant sales and marketing representative, while Ms. Paluka is his junior senior assistant, they get down to work. They prepare carefully, even exhaustively, for the meeting the next day with the big client. After a break for a room-service omelet with a crisp and somewhat reckless Chardonnay, she takes off her trim jacket, and suddenly feels wonderfully vulnerable, yet powerful and womanly in her white silk blouse.

Out with the laptop computers and the other stuff!

Time passes remarkably quickly when one is exhausting one's self with demanding tasks in the unforgiving yet electrically charged world of microchips!

Mr. Pepp glances at Ms. Paluka's breasts, breasts that slowly, and despite her M.B.A. from Stanford, heave, beneath the lustrous and creamy silk of her blouse. She pretends not to notice, and yet, a faint flush starts at her neck and rises swiftly toward her ears. How she wished she had a cigarette! Yet she had heeded the Surgeon General's warnings and given them up several years ago. That Techmaxcon did not permit smoking, even in the immaculate parking lot, had had something to do with it. Thanks a million, Techmaxcon!, she often breathed. She could actually smell the *gas!*

"Looks as if we've more or less got this baby *locked* up, Ms. Paluka. Now if we can start out on the same page with old Tromboner tomorrow, and convince him that our new hard-drive soft-disc microparticle floppy byte-generator is what his expanding business needs, I think that we should both be headed back to home base with smiles on our faces, and the guys' applause awaiting us! (At Techmaxcon, all the employees were called "guys," by common consent. There had been some grumbling about this at first, but a few motivational weekends of drumming and "jungle combat" had put everyone, at the end of the day, on the same page.)

She looks down at the traffic far below the hotel room window, the lights reflected in a dozen gleaming colors on the rain-slick streets. *This* is what it was all about! What an odd name Tromboner is, she muses. Perhaps he's an ethnic person, an Eyetalian, they tend to have very strange foreign names, and so hard to *pronounce!* Russo. Zito. Gallo. Lupo. She couldn't even think how to say them. Whew!

Earlier, in a nicely familiar flashback, it has been revealed that Ms. Paluka's ex-husband, Brad, had tried every trick in the book to keep her from getting her M.B.A., even going so far as to insult Palo Alto. And how she wanted a child! Yet Brad, soft, pouting, selfish Brad, would not hear of sharing household tasks, and as for taking care of a baby while she attended her demanding classes, ha!

Certainly it wouldn't hurt to have a bottle of Cognac sent up to the room! "A few snifters before bed won't spoil us." He was quite the rogue, Mr. Pepp was, and Ms. Paluka was beginning to understand why he had called the office volleyball team, "the Tex-Maxies." He was just so fun!

"You're not trying to get me tipsy, are you, Mishter Russho?"

"What?"

Oh dear, she'd forgotten his name for a moment, and knew that the Five Star V.S.O.P. Cognac, Hennesshy's, had gone to her head. And yet, the boiling turmoil in her heaving breasts also had something to do with the emotion that filled her womanly being. But she was a junior senior assistant, for God's sake!

"Quite all right, Ms. Paluka, even I'd forget my name if it weren't attached to my shoulders, ha ha." This Mr. Pepp is one heck of a good sport. Ms. Paluka feels a certain tingle as he becomes serious and notes, hesitantly, that he couldn't help but notice her looking down at the traffic far below on the rain-slicked streets, and he'd been in enough lonely hotel rooms to know what *that* means.

Oh, oh, what *did* it mean!? Did she dare ask?

"By the way, Ms. Paluka, I—"

"You may call me Aspen . . . if . . . you l-l-like."

"Aspen. Well, then, Aspen. I have been meaning to tell you that my infant son, Brett—I find this difficult to speak of, even now—that Brett died in infancy of an undiagnosed mystery disease."

"Oh, Mister Zito, I mean, Peppo, no! No!"

Of course, his marriage has never been the same, his wife blames him for the child's death, since the death occurred while he was entertaining a client, a big client, at the Grand Opera. And it turned out, oh, how strange fate can be, despite exercise and a sensible diet, that he didn't like opera and the account was lost. The irony almost overwhelmed Mister Jerry Pepp, a man whom irony rarely troubled.

"Don't . . . don't cry, Mr. Pepp, Mr.—darling," Aspen whispers, as she slips out of her clothes, blouse first, her eager breasts heaving sensually. "Come, come to my arms."

And then the singing of the larks and nightingales burst forth over the shrouded dreamed-of moors as their voices soared into the cerulean blue that covered the ocean pounding again and again and again . . .

Is Mr. Pepp lying, and does Aspen Paluka care whether he is or not? Doesn't Ms. Paluka, intelligent and attractive at thirty-five or so, deserve to eat the pâté, drink the cocktails, earn the big salary, make the bonus money, get the nookie? Doesn't she deserve to read the latest books by the writers who wish to share their demanding thoughts on modern life in a clear and simple yet colorful style? Of course! Life, Ms. Paluka knows, is not just silk blouses and bras that fit right.

Note: Feel of bedspread. Lights from traffic far below on walls of room. Distant foghorns from the dark sea beyond the sleepless metropolis. Brief description of Mr. Pepp's sadness as he muses on his little cabin in Vermont, a cabin that Mrs. Pepp has always hated, hated the fish and the beavers and the coots and the firewood, no, she preferred to stay at home in the comfort of their luxury co-op overlooking the Golden Gate. He was, then, always alone in the woods, with the deerflies and the wasps and the smell of skunk in the air and the splash of trout in the clear cold water, alone with his sad thoughts of Brett and his fading dreams . . .

"I LOVE Vermont!," Aspen laughs. And it turns out that her Dad was a Forest Ranger in the Smokies and that she was, dammit!, almost weaned on jerky and hogjowl and boiled beans. Her Dad had a dream of the World Wide Web once, and had met Jack Kerouac.

They fall asleep in each other's arms, and Aspen thanks her lucky stars that she thought hard about her important night-clothes selection so carefully. As the women liked to joke over that first cup of decaf, you never can tell when your boss will want to interact on a warm, personal level with you.

■   ■   ■

The author, at a loss to come up with anything new to say about the world of business (with which he is obviously unacquainted, and, grievously, unwilling to research), has apparently dumped the contents of some notebook scribblings onto the page and is hoping to pass it off as "innovative" literature. Not surprisingly, he is probably wholly unfamiliar with Gertrude Stein's comment on *Finnigan's Wake,* "The quarks are not literature." Cryptic, so to say, yes, but true.

"She might be right about the notebook, Jerry."

Prudence Rydstrom, battling her way into an Ooh-La-La French-lace-trimmed semitransparent peekaboo long-line torsolette with detachable brassiere, dayglo faux-bustier, six patent-leather semi-detachable garters with neon insets, and a battery-powered combination dildo/cocktail shaker, says that all the girls—even, believe it or not, her sister, Maxine—agree with her that Mr. Pepp and Ms. Paluka make a loving and romantic couple and that they deserve a little fucking happiness.

"So long as the gentleman employs a rubber on himself so as not to communicate an unwanted clap to the lady's shameful parts," Mary Connors, R.N., says. "It's only right. Not that I make an implication that the gentleman has got himself a nice little dose, but you can't be too careful nowadays, what with people copulating here, there, and everywhere, and with perfect strangers who could be festering with dread carnal diseases. We see a lot of it in our business."

"Oh, these lovely ladies! Altogether," Mr. Joyce says, "a scherza-rade of one's thousand one nightinesses. And perhaps you might check to be sure you've transcribed *this* correctly?"

[The decision to include this chapter in the work that became *Little Casino* was not easily arrived at. It was initially felt that the author['s] "style" and approach were not commensurate with that of the rest of the work. Ultimately, if reluctantly, that view was modified, on the ground that "the content outweighs the . . . deficiencies of execution."]

SHE WORRIED ABOUT CIGARETTE SMOKING, cigarette smokers, and, most especially, secondhand cigarette smoke that might well be everywhere, virtually invisible, some of it lurking in corners and near baseboards for decades, and about the fact that those exposed to this smoke, either directly or indirectly, had little or no idea of what to do about nuclear waste. She fretted about all the wonderful, intelligent dolphins that were killed along with all the marvelous, beautiful tuna, and that the callous and unenlightened fishermen who slaughtered them would, if they stopped slaughtering them, stay home on welfare collecting their fat checks and drinking beer all day. She was concerned that a well-spoken legal secretary, who had been complimented on her attractiveness by her boss, a man with absolute power over her career, had been plunged into near-psychosis by this occurrence, and that the boss had compounded his offense by persistently suggesting to the hapless woman that it was perfectly all right for persons in good health to eat as many as five eggs a week. She was upset that a CEO who had always seemed like a wonderful man with his big white smile and deep voice and his concern for hungry children in Somantia or Rguanda or someplace hot and dirty had left his wife of thirty-two years, a wonderful woman who played tennis and was always tan, for a twenty-three-year-old California woman described as a "Palo Alto yogurt therapist and relationship coach," and that neither of them seemed to be alarmed in the least that suggestive dancing in public seemed to be on the rise. She often lay awake at night thinking of the bothersome homoerotic behavior displayed by athletes of both sexes while engaged in their various sporting pursuits, and that not a single one of them had ever spoken out about the impossibility of convicting a black millionaire of anything, since they not only get all the breaks, they also get everything handed to them on a silver platter. She stewed silently when she came to realize that not one single president in her lifetime had possessed the courage to speak out against really short skirts in places of business, since fashion designers are all homosexuals, who not only get all the breaks, but they also get everything handed to them on a silver platter. She was disgruntled because of the possibility that chicken offered for sale in seemingly clean markets might be contaminated with salmonella, some kind of Arab disease invented by Saddam Hussein, yet careless butchers, even after all these years, show no interest in really excellent books that tell good stories, but prefer to look at dirty pictures back in the refrigerator. She was considerably troubled by the fact that no amount of washing could ever rid fruit of deadly insecticides imported from Iran or someplace like that by the liberals in Congress, and she knew in her heart that the badly paid Mexicans who sprayed the fruit were also shooting wolves and coyotes, when they could spare a moment from their enchiladas and tequila and urinating in the streets, or *calles*. She hated the loggers who spent much of their days ravaging the forests of this once-beautiful land, and was certainly not at all surprised to learn that they were wholly unconcerned about the high levels of caffeine in the soft drinks that their children seem to like so much. She became very nervous about secondhand cigar smoke, and was appalled to learn, from her daily newspaper's Health and You section, that most cigar smoke has a carcinogenic half-life of 40,000 years, the same as refined sugar. She was enraged that none of those exposed to this smoke, although possibly rendered sterile, bothered to discover for themselves that the Jews, who owned the entertainment business, the banks, the beer companies and spirits distilleries and newspapers, the television stations, the Empire State Building, the Golden Gate Bridge, 51% of Alabama, Harvard, and the NAACP, also owned all the cigar factories in Communist Cuba, whence all these fashionable cancer-rolls come from, despite the lies of the Jewish-owned, liberal-socialist-neoconservative press and its kept columnists, all of whom have changed their "kosher" names. She was filled with anxiety when she discovered that the Boards of Directors of dozens, not to say scores, of this once-proud nation's most powerful companies were made up of Satanists, Muslim fundamentalists, or both, and that the stockholders of these corporations had no idea that demonically possessed-and-directed great white sharks kill just as many dolphins and tuna as do drunken New England fishermen, although many of these aquatic wonders of nature are also destroyed by chewing-tobacco sputum carelessly deposited in streams and rivers by Jewish farmers and baseball players. She was discouraged to find that ranchers love to shoot weasels, which they callously call "barn coyotes," but somewhat soothed when informed that these same weasels lust to kill, and kill savagely, newborn lambs and bunnies. She could barely countenance the revelation that those charged with controlling the predations of the demonic great white sharks were discovered to be more interested in establishing the rights of homosexuals to perform disgusting sex acts with and on each other anywhere they please, but especially in public schools. When it came to homosexuals, or "homos," as, she learned, they prefer to call themselves, she was really astonished when informed that almost every single Hollywood star, even the big strong men, is a "homo," and yet no one who was aware of this was concerned in the least as to why country music is no longer really *country* music, but an invention of African American ghetto persons, believe it or not! And although she had no idea why jazz, even by African American persons who really know how to play it, like that Winston Margolis, is supposed to be so good, she felt a little ashamed of herself for sometimes wishing that they'd play some nice, familiar, good old comfortable rock and roll. She sobbed with anger at the news of the .229 lifetime hitter who had signed a three-year contract for twenty-eight million dollars, with an incentive clause promising an additional one hundred thousand dollars for every point over .229 in each of the three seasons, especially when he boasted that he'd celebrate with "a big, thick steak, a cigar, and my friend, the journalist Candace Herbert-Mills." She was doubtful that the United States Army is a violent organization, but shocked to learn that a survey of non-commissioned officers named one of television news's most vivacious, wholesome, and courageously hard-hitting personalities "a piece of ass." She was beside herself with frustration when she read that some of her taxes would possibly be used to care for the skin cancers of those who insisted on their tans each summer, and who, bronze-gold glowing, were utterly passive in the face of malt-liquor consumption in the inner city, especially in the doorways of welfare offices. Still, she was somewhat surprised to be apprised of the probability that poor and powerless people, especially of dark skin, are sometimes treated with rudeness, force, and even brutality by police officers, not one of whom cares about the very high levels of LDL cholesterol in crisp chicken skin. Did that really likeable actor, the sunny, slightly chubby one with the lopsided grin, know how upset she was when he left his wife because of the orgies that the poor woman was forced to take part in by a famous producer, who just happens to be an adept at Jewish black magic? She had, too, been sobered by the article in a national news magazine that detailed the high rates of venality, boredom, envy, cruelty, greed, and just plain dumbness among gay persons, or "homos," virtually all of whom were on record as adoring disco dancing, washed-up divas, pastel colors, really bad musicals, and blondes. And the cowboy who left his businesswoman wife of fifty-three for a surfer girl shocked her, especially when he confessed that he ate a double cheeseburger every day. And although she resisted the notion as best she could, it seemed to her that there was something to the accusation that girls in short skirts were, well, "asking for it," despite their Buddhist beliefs, whole grains, and yoga exercises. She was just livid at the lack of respect, shown by swarthy welfare cheats and their shyster Jewish lawyers, for good Christian beliefs, like charity and Jesus Christ. And speaking of disrespect, certain ethnic and religious types were perfectly happy to criticize evangelical preachers and those who had been reborn, yet had no suggestions for frustrating or delaying the revival of restricting and constraining foundation garments. She was made uncomfortable by teenage boys, and was not in the least surprised to find that they had never heard of Custer's Last Stand, the Monkees, Brian Wilson, or Peter Fonda, let alone Barry Manilow and Anne Tyler.

There were, surely, other things that worried, concerned, angered, appalled, and enraged her, but she continued to use Sunset Blush lipstick because her really manly but gentlemanly Italian American boss had once made a subtle and charmingly suggestive comment on her mouth, and she also continued to consume Ho-Hos, although they reminded her of an unpleasant summer she had spent at Camp Gitchegumee. She ate three meals a day, dieted constantly, was warm in winter and cool in summer, and had a number of so-so friends who were not curious or demanding or intrusive or constant. She thought her sex life a disaster, although it was, more or less, the norm. All in all, she lived better than eighty-five percent of the human beings on the face of this indifferent earth.

■ ■ ■

And when the winter arrives for this concerned and worried woman, why, let it snow, let it snow, let it snow.

"Well, if Jewish persons, and I'll be the first, believe me, to say that you've gotta hand it to them, if they don't own all the news media, how do you explain the fact that Rex Morgan, M.D., changed his name from Morgansky?"

Uh-huh.

This woman once owned a pale-blue knitted dress, but a person or persons unknown broke into her apartment and cut the dress into one-inch strips. A note, which read, in its entirety, "Dunderbeck's Machine," was left beneath her Christmas tree, long stripped of ornaments and lights, and thoroughly dried out.

(Might be a symbol.)

Mr. Schmitz writes: "There will be a tremendous explosion, but no one will hear it and the earth will return to its nebulous state and go wandering through the sky, free at last from parasites and disease."

"Mr. Schmitz was Jewish and changed *his* name."

N MOTHER'S DAY SHE TAKES HER MOTHER to the Paris on 58th Street to see Olivier's *Hamlet*. Afterward, they go to Rumpelmayer's for ice cream and coffee, and then stroll over to the Plaza and then down Fifth Avenue. All these small, thoughtful, and seemingly loving acts are really instances of an anemic contempt for and patronization of her mother, who, she is sure, absolutely sure, would much rather have seen a Bette Davis double feature in the neighborhood rerun house, the Stanley, and then have enjoyed a melted-cheese sandwich and a cup of tea in Holsten's Ice-Cream Parlor. Her mother had little to say about the movie other than a comment on Olivier's bleached hair. Well, why *would* she even begin to understand it? Her mother had gone to Manual Training High School, and was unaccountably proud of the commercial diploma that she had earned. God! They walk down to 34th Street, chatting and window-shopping, and then prepare to separate, she to board a bus for the Village, her mother to take the subway to Bay Ridge.

Thanks, her mother says, so much, thanks so much, sweetie, I really enjoyed our day, it was such a nice surprise. They stand and wait for the daughter's bus, which is just down the avenue, and her mother kisses her on the cheek and moves away. Really wonderful, dear, she says, so lovely to be up near the Plaza again, it's been such a long time, and I remembered the hotel, too, perfectly. Talk about a long time! What? her daughter says. The Plaza, her mother says, the beautiful Plaza and the week I spent there, oh, long before I was pregnant with you. A couple of thousand years ago. What? her daughter says, and then she gets on the bus, and as she sits down, sees her mother walking west down the street, heading for the subway.

The Plaza? A week at the Plaza? And before she was pregnant. Her father was not the sort of man who would take her mother to the *Plaza*. A week alone at the Plaza? Why? She sees, in her mind's eye, her mother as a young woman. This is intolerable. She'll call her tonight. A week at the Plaza, but not with her father, surely not. She must have misunderstood her mother, she was always doing that. Did she say a beautiful week?

■   ■   ■

Children are often surprised to learn that before their births their parents lived secret, complex lives from which these children are wholly excluded. There they are in old photographs, dressed in odd clothes, their curiously unfamiliar faces in the foreground of strange streets and obsolete automobiles. This young woman, for instance, thinks of her mother in her remodeled gray Persian lamb coat, or sitting down to a plate of cream of chicken soup in the Bay Terrace Lounge and Restaurant, or scrambling eggs while she sings "Poor Butterfly." What she cannot imagine is her mother, her clothes in disarray, being fucked from behind by a lover.

"I think, although I only caught a quick glimpse of these women, that the older one might have been Annette."

The older woman was not Annette, but Linda Piro. Had she been Annette, there would have been here proffered a clean juxtaposition, across time and space, of two different years and two different parks. I might even have had the pleasure of seeing Annette, once again, holding down her light beige skirt, which the wind is lifting, slightly, above her knees. Oh well, another time, perhaps.

The young woman, Linda's daughter, Isabelle, has been dead for many years, as you know.

Small magic

E TELLS, YET AGAIN, WITH A LITTLE ADDED here and a little subtracted there, a story centered on Fat Harry, an essentially unremarkable story, tells it as if to understand what he may think of as a "secret" at its banal core. Fat Harry of angry, abused, neglected, and deserted wives and forgotten children, of bad debts and beatings by shylocks and policy muscle, of absurdly long shots with no chance to run in the money, of disastrous losing streaks created and sustained by betting the wrong way, the right way, the hard way, by drawing to inside straights, holding low kickers, bluffing with pairs of deuces and treys, ignoring aces up, betting carefully when winning and recklessly when losing. In short, a chump. A Fat Harry of drunken nights and gonorrhea, lost keys, back rent, wrecked and repossessed cars, broken windows, maudlin tears, filthy bathrooms, dirty underwear, take-out Chinese, useless refrigerators leaking freon, plastic forks and spoons, dull knives, semen-spattered girlie magazines, of this job and that job, moving furniture, painting shotgun flats, spraying roaches and bedbugs,

helping out in saloons in Bay Ridge and Park Slope, Red Hook and Borough Park, Greenpoint and Bath Beach. A Fat Harry who cleans out urinals, mops up vomit and blood, washes grease-slick dishes, walks dogs, shovels coal and snow, washes cars, pumps gas, delivers dry cleaning and laundry and groceries and flowers and pizza. A Fat Harry of fruitless, hopeless, futile, irrational, meaningless journeys by bus to Scranton and Wilkes-Barre, to Wilmington, Richmond, Albany, to Altoona and Camden, to the Delaware Water Gap, to the Poconos, to Binghamton and Paterson, for what reason? For no reason, for any reason, to be able to say—nothing. Nothing at all. A Fat Harry who is punched in the mouth and nose, who suffers lacerations and abrasions, cracked teeth, a broken jaw, crushed ribs, sprained fingers, split lips, for talking, for not talking, for saying the wrong thing, for not answering, for making promises and breaking promises, for being a wiseass, for being a dummy, for being a momo, for just being fucking there. A Fat Harry, who, in some crazed final gesture before he disappeared, trailing bad markers and murderous bookmakers, used his temporary night bartender job to close the Lucky Shamrock Bar and Grill, a police hangout by day and early evening, at 3:00 A.M. of a Saturday morning, to pull the blinds so as to enable the dozen patrons still at the bar to drink free of charge, dance to the jukebox fed by the bar's quarters, laugh and embrace and sing and kiss and grope each other, make drunken assignations, confess hidden attractions, and then stagger out of the joint at dawn, reeling and blinking and joyous in the thin cold of the pre-snow morning, ecstatic with the pleasure of transgression. I'm fucking dead anyway, Harry supposedly said, by way of explanation, as he pocketed the cash in the till. And so he probably was.

■   ■   ■

Fat Harry was the vector of small magic, the profane and secular equivalent of the sinner chosen by God to be the conduit of grace.

Grace, by the way, was the name of one of Fat Harry's sad, mistreated wives.

It is an urban rule of thumb that police hangouts are good places to stay away from, at least while officers of the law are on the premises. This, in spite of the fact that the policeman is our friend.

It may be clear that this Fat Harry is not the same Fat Harry who died* in the oily waters off the Brooklyn Navy Yard.

* *Vide* "Presidential Greetings."

BUT WHAT ARE THE STEPS OF THE PROOF that inevitably concludes that there are no winter wonderlands here, no deep purple, falling or otherwise, no stardust or star eyes or sleigh bells or open fires or garden walls or angels singing? Shall we accept the conclusions of such a proof without insisting on a clarification of its steps; or, at the very least, a dry martini? And although it *may* be proved that the light of bowling alleys is romantic, it must be made clear that those bowling alleys are nowhere in this vicinity, brother! And if Cheech and Nickie marry Annette and Inez, that will in no way enable those bowling alleys, to, well, appear. Nor will it preclude the vomiting of black blood by old men, dying in little pieces from bad food, bad whiskey, bad luck, and humiliation, their hearts more or less broken; nor will such ecstatic couplings improve the ratio of tapioca to semen in reprehensible masculine dreams, dreams in which young women are treated with the utmost disrespect, ruthlessly undressed, and spoken to in language not fit for a barracks, and there isn't much that is not fit for a barracks, and all this carried out within the very dreamwork itself! A person could die from embarrassment. So Freud is wrong, yet again, thanks be to God. And after the light of bowling alleys has been used to "help one get through life's daily stresses," what apologist for the shameless fraud of a shambling Viennese Jew, whom dimmest sophomores can smugly mock, will dare to attempt to prove that he was less a fraud than Georgia O'Keefe, whose least accomplished paintings are moreso, oh moreso than they ever were, scintillant in their location, insistent in the depth of a statement that controls the picture plane with the saturated colors that are certain in their regard for the iconoclasm of erotic love, and twice on Sunday. Like chicken and mashed potatoes and fresh peas, with a full gravy boat down at the end of the table. Hey, pass that down, OK, Georgia? And who first noted that Ms. O'Keefe once said that she painted well on Saturdays but badly on Sundays, chock full as she inevitably was with "chicken and taters," as she affectedly called the dish? It was, never doubt it for a moment, somebody. That's exactly the way things used to be in old Santa Fe, a town that can never be imitated, nor even vaguely suggested as to its color, shade, and charm around these parts, dear pal. And it's a cinch that not one resident would tolerate for a moment an imitation—assuming such an unlikely horror—of the town that is often called "prettier than Frisco." These residents, or representative samplings of same, would, instead, make their way to the Loew's Alpine to see a double feature with such actors as George Brent, Veronica Lake, Rondo Hatton, Edward Arnold, and Jack Carson, plus coming attractions, cartoons, a Pete Smith Specialty, a Robert Benchley short, and the news.

The Alpine took to sporting blue sateen banners, which, draped casually from its marquee, announced, in silver letters, that the theater was AIR COOLED BY FRIGIDAIRE. Many have tried, oh many, many have tried in vain to prove that the blue of the banner was the blue of Lake Como or Lake Tahoe or Lake Sapphire, or even, for that matter, Lake Hopatcong, but there's no chance of such a serene and glamorous lacustrine blue existing around here, sport. You have, by the way, an honest face, something like Jack Carson's.

■ ■ ■

Alfred Stieglitz, or so they say, wrote letters to Georgia O'Keefe in which he said more amorous, even erotic things, in barracks language, than you can shake a stick at. Nothing, by the way, is "prettier than Frisco," often called "the Santa Fe of California," whatever that means. Nothing.

Jack Carson, who regularly played loud fools whose bonhomie could not conceal—nor was it meant to—the larceny in their hearts, had an uncanny ability to let the audience see his tender vulnerability beneath the intentionally revealed cupidity and the hearty bluster, so that when he was on screen, one watched three people at once. He can be seen at work in many films, two of his best being *Strawberry Blonde* and *Mildred Pierce*.

"They don't make 'em like Jack Carson anymore," Fat George the Armenian says. "Now any dimwitted dumb fuck of an actor is a STAR! You could die laughing." His father, filling a huge jar on the counter of his Italian-Greek Food Products store, adds, "Bill Harris's dozen or so choruses on his 'In a Mellotone' are worth any five movie stars you can think of, male or female. Hell, they're worth any five Nobel laureates you can think of!"

Had Freud somehow known that Gloria Steinem once "worked" as a Playboy Bunny in order to get "material" for a "story," would he have remarked: "Uh-huh" or "Worked?" or "An anal repressive, surely" or "Not a bad built, Klaus"?

George's father filled the huge jar with, let's say, Greek olives.

Barracks language is always everywhere vile, and yet, after a time, it takes on the homely qualities of security, familiarity, and, generally speaking, regulated domesticity.

"That is no fucking lie, you sorry sonofabitch motherfucker," Corporal Wing avers, looking up from his fucking field-fucking-stripped M-1 carbine. Home sweet fucking home.

IS MIND NO LONGER SEEMS TO FUNCTION properly, or, in any event, efficiently, but has become, instead, a welter of discrete images, all of which have equal importance. This eccentricity may not stand him in good stead, as they used to say, given the no-nonsense lust for instant results and useful facts that drives the nation. Well. He cannot, or will not, organize or categorize experiences. So that although he may recall the time that he first kissed a girl, and although his recollection that it occurred at another girl's fifteenth birthday party is probably correct, he cannot see himself at that party as other than the seventeen-year-old who lost his virginity in the park situated just two blocks from the house in which the party was held. The name of the girl he kissed was Helen Ryan; the name of the girl in the park was Constance Mangini. Kisses, he remembers, somebody's kisses, that tasted of vanilla. His entire past seems to work, if that's the word, this way now, so that sometimes he knows that he kissed Constance at the party and pulled up Helen's thrilling skirt under

a tree in Bliss Park. And who is that little boy, or is it that gray-haired old man, who is falling in with his company at Fort Hood? He doesn't seem to mind this confusion of the temporal, this shifting of imagery, this aphasia of blurred time. It fits, it seems to him, rather well with the blood-drenched, always justified chaos of the collapsing century's history, its legacy, God help us all. Once in a while he feels his own flesh, still reasonably sound, firmly fixed in long-gone time, and he turns to smile at people who are dead. The ravishing taste of a Lucky Strike as the war ends in the Pacific, the smell of his first love's sun-warm skin, a clear picture of a woman, desired and desiring, on a shady patio, in white summer clothes, her gin and tonic lifted in a toast to something wholly forgotten but sweet, surely sweet. And who is that drunken soldier in dirty khakis and a flowered shirt on the street in Waco, of all places, a sandwich in one hand and a pint of J.W. Dant in the other?

■ ■ ■

I'm afraid the two girls mentioned in this putatively tender yet wholly pointless, if not useless "recollection" have had their names garbled. They were Constance Ryan and Helen Mangini. The former was the recipient of what she now thinks of as the "unwelcome sexual attentions" addressed to her in the park. Constance was wearing a blue-and-white-striped linen skirt, and was concerned lest grass stains suggest to her brother, Paulie, an amorous dalliance. He put his jacket down for her when she said that she didn't want Paulie to find out about it. Find out about what? he said, his hand under that tight skirt.

"They don't much go in for Dant in California, as far as I can see, am I right? You never hear it mentioned."

"Well, whiskey and cigarettes will kill you in about twenty minutes in California, a well-known fact. The only things that won't hurt you are the merciless sunshine and the thousands of tons of poisonous automobile emissions that daily add a certain spice to the pollen and mold in the air. Anyway, 'some weather!' is a useful phrase to keep in readiness amid the friendly hollow smiles."

(Another useful phrase is "how do you like San Francisco?" The reply should be either "compared to what?" or "it's the Queens of California.")

The true name of Bliss Park is Owl's Head Park, by which appellation it is never called, at least not by neighborhood residents. The tree under which the young lovers performed their inexpert sexual acts was a rare copper beech. The tree may still be in the park.

Maybe Frisco is the Waco of California.

"Paulie was *Helen's* brother!"

Hi!

We're in the city that's often called the Waco of California, but it looks sort of like Queens. Some weather! We've been reading about all the snow back home, ha ha. We'll bring you back a souvenir from Haight-Ashbury where they invented modern beatnik poetry and rock and roll.

Love, Helen and Connie

E HAS ON NAVY BLUE WOOLEN TRUNKS, cinched by a white canvas belt with a tarnished nickel-plated buckle, and a white cotton athletic-style shirt, on the chest of which is embroidered a navy-blue anchor to echo the embroidered white anchor on the right leg of his trunks. His mother and grandfather are with him, as are two teenage girls, Helen and Julia Carpenter. They have small breasts, which he looks at surreptitiously as often as he can, the little degenerate. Mr. Jenivere and his weirdly corpselike wife sit on an adjoining blanket. Mr. Jenivere considers himself to be "quite a croquet player," elegant and ruthless, but his grandfather beats him, daily, without, as they say, half trying, and he compounds this indignity by playing the sweet, quiet game with a careless air, one of studied distraction, as if Mr. Jenivere is not really worth his concentration. The air off the lake is cool, and the leaves on the trees that cluster around the chalk-white casino crackle slightly with early messages of autumn. His mother takes him to the casino and they sit in the

taproom, where she orders a Tom Collins for herself and an orangeade for him. She gives him a sip of her Collins from its magical frosted glass, and lights a Herbert Tareyton. The taste of the gin and lemon, the fragrant cigarette smoke, are, oh yes, appurtenances of leisure and summer, of the complex world of adulthood. A man at the bar, dressed in a pale-green polo shirt and white slacks and shoes, turns slightly on his bar stool and looks at his mother's legs.

Dolores lies on the blanket next to him and her thigh, her warm, smooth flesh, touches his. Her hair is so black that it shines in the sunlight with deep blue and dark red glints. Her buttocks are round and perfect in her yellow bathing suit, whose little skirt completely and erotically subverts its purported function of modest concealment. He bites the flesh of his forearm to calm his longing. Hopelessly shaken by lust, he fights against a surrender to impure thoughts, however inaccurate their images may be.

The jukebox in the pavilion was playing a song that would, of course, be freighted with poignancy in years to come. I had a feeling you weren't going to come, she said. How could she think that? It was obvious, from his stupid, beaming, stricken face that he was captive and slave to her, that he would be, forever, should she wish it, her chump and patsy. She was sitting on the blanket, her forearms crossed on her knees, squinting up at him, her face in a nimbus of honey-colored hair. Her thighs were slightly open, and he smiled vapidly, staring at her chin. Well, I'm here, he said. Here I am. The fucking dimwit idiot.

They played gin on the blanket, the cards sticky from the salt wind, the sun beginning to go down, the beach almost empty of people, the lifeguards packing up their gear. The children were cold, and clustered together in their sweatshirts, wrapped in a blanket, giggling and chanting a word that had struck them funny. He finished the last of the vodka and orange juice, and asked Ben if he wanted to play another hand, but it really was getting late. His wife sat, some few yards from the water's edge, watching the ocean tumbling in ragged echelons, as she'd done for the last three hours. The bitch. Go get your wife and let's go home, Ben said, as he handed his wife the folded blankets and the plastic cooler and thermos. Are we ready?, his wife said. *All* of us? He got up and called to his wife, then began walking toward her with her denim skirt and worn sandals under his arm. She turned around but looked, not at him, but toward the children. He thought that maybe he should just throw her fucking clothes at her and take the bus home. Or somewhere.

The day was terribly hot and windless, and the sun on the Sound was so bright that it hurt their eyes. This was not a day to be at the beach, especially this pebble beach, which seemed hotter than sand. She was exquisite, glowing dark gold in her black one-piece suit, and he asked her if she wanted to swim, but she said that she just wanted to get wet and go back to the cottage. We can take our lunch back and eat on the patio. Under the trees, the lovely shady trees. They went into the water and then packed up quickly and walked the half-mile back to the cottage. Inside it was dim and cool. Shall we take a shower before we eat?, she said. Sure, he said, and pulled his trunks down, half-turning away from her. Well, look at *you*, she said. He blushed. It must be the heat, he said, unless it's the company. She pulled the straps of her bathing suit down and began to strip it off. What do we say, handsome, to the beach? The suit was around her dark-gold thighs, and she stood still and looked at him. We say, he said, you beautiful tomato, Farewell beach, Hello shower! Come on and do some dirty things to me, she said, I love you, God knows why.

■　■　■

There are additional lakeside and oceanside scenes that might have been here included to strengthen the figures of love desired, love burgeoning, and love dying, but the stern demands of organic form must be met, and I am, most of the time, the man to meet them. And since love's magic spell is everywhere, dear reader, you may add your own remarks or amorous aquatic memories in, perhaps, the margins.

However, be cognizant of the fact that remarks are not literature, as Sylvia Plath once read.

"Nor are amorous aquatic memories," Miss Stein says.

Budd Lake, Lake Hopatcong, Lake Hiawatha, Lake Ronkonkoma, Riis Park, Jones Beach, Coney Island. That's the ticket!

"Those are not even remarks."

"The turn of the wave and the scutter of receding pebbles."

"Poluphloisboio thalassa."

"Pollyfizzyboisterous."

Then, of course, speaking of beaches, you have Gerty McDowell, sweet, yearning, lascivious, lame Gerty. That's another ticket.

"You'll never know," Mr. Bloom, yet another beachgoer, mutters.

THE BUDD LAKE CASINO IS A DAZZLING citadel in the summer sunlight. It is set back, in its gleaming whiteness, from a pale-golden beach, and offers shade and coolness, and the glamour of rattled ice in silvery cocktail shakers, the romantic smell of whiskey and bitters, lemon, and cigarette smoke, and the easy, crisp swing of white big bands on the jukebox. The tunes say, again and again, "peace," as if the sudden ebbing of the Depression has come about without a price to be paid. The casino was not really like this, as you surely will know, save to a boy of twelve, and by the time he wanted to know just what it *was* like, it was gone, and the people who could tell him the truth, or, perhaps, their truth, were dead. So it exists, a white dream, "whose terraces are the color of stars."

■　■　■

A casino is a "little house."

"Little casino" is a neat tautology.

Hoyle, on the card game, Casino: "Suits are of no importance."

And yet, in the game, a Little Casino is the Two of Spades, and is worth one point. Such contradictions and blithe disruptions are the stuff of poetry.

Like many other things, the game is no longer in fashion. Just as well. There are many instances and objects of value and beauty that should be kept private, even secret. For instance, it is surely all for the best that perhaps fifty people in the world know the author of:

Take me back to the days
Of an old walnetto song
To a walnetto blonde
That pinned the white blossoms over the bosom,
and pulled at the heart's strings of the world.

Selah.

Other Books by Gilbert Sorrentino

BIBLIOGRAPHY

Gilbert Sorrentino: A Descriptive Bibliography

POETRY

The Darkness Surrounds Us
Black and White
The Perfect Fiction
Corrosive Sublimate
A Dozen Oranges
Sulpiciae Elegidia: Elegiacs of Sulpicia
White Sail
The Orangery
Selected Poems 1958-1980

FICTION

The Sky Changes
Steelwork
Imaginative Qualities of Actual Things
Flawless Play Restored: The Masque of Fungo
Splendide-Hôtel
Mulligan Stew
Aberration of Starlight
Crystal Vision
Blue Pastoral
Odd Number
A Beehive Arranged on Humane Principles
Rose Theatre
Misterioso
Under the Shadow
Red the Fiend
Pack of Lies
Gold Fools

ESSAYS

Something Said

Colophon

Little Casino was designed at Coffee House Press
in the Warehouse District of downtown Minneapolis.
The text is set in Caslon with Protege titles.

Good books are brewing at coffeehousepress.org